NUMBER SEARCH

TIMES TABLES

Over 80 fun multiplication and division puzzles!

ARCTURUS

TIMES TABLES GRID

0	1	2	3	4	5	6	7	8	9	10	11	12
1	1	2	3	4	5	6	7	8	9	10	11	12
2	2	4	6	8	10	12	14	16	18	20	22	24
3	3	6	9	12	15	18	21	24	27	30	33	36
4	4	8	12	16	20	24	28	32	36	40	44	48
5	5	10	15	20	25	30	35	40	45	50	55	60
6	6	12	18	24	30	36	42	48	54	60	66	72
7	7	14	21	28	35	42	49	56	63	70	77	84
8	8	16	24	32	40	48	56	64	72	80	88	96
9	9	18	27	36	45	54	63	72	81	90	99	108
10	10	20	30	40	50	60	70	80	90	100	110	120
11	11	22	33	44	55	66	77	88	99	110	121	132
12	12	24	36	48	60	72	84	96	108	120	132	144

All the equations come from the 1 to 12 times tables. Use this grid to help if you get stuck.

ARCTURUS
This edition published in 2021 by Arcturus Publishing Limited
26/27 Bickels Yard, 151–153 Bermondsey Street,
London SE1 3HA

Author: Annabel Savery
Illustrator: Jess Bradley
Cover illustrator: Susana Gurrea
Editor: Becca Clunes
Designer: Stefan Holliland
Editorial manager: Joe Harris

ISBN: 987-1-3988-0401-2
CH008628NT
Supplier 29, Date 0521, Print run 11577

Printed in China

HOW TO USE THIS BOOK

Hello times tables detectives, we're on the hunt for some equations. Are you ready to search? Grab your pencil and let's get started!

At the top of each page is information to tell you what skills you'll need to solve the puzzle.

On each page you will find a grid like this one:

5	7	x	−	÷	−	−	−	9	5	1
−	8	3	+	x	x	5	6	=	6	3
2	÷	5	+	7	+	2	1	0	÷	1
÷	÷	6	+	3	4	=	=	1	+	3
7	6	7	4	0	5	5	2	÷	8	2
8	8	4	−	2	7	x	÷	0	3	3
4	1	=	2	x	7	5	2	9	0	÷
9	x	9	−	1	6	8	6	÷	2	0
7	x	1	0	=	7	0	5	÷	1	7
7	2	8	x	8	+	=	2	5	2	6
7	9	4	0	6	6	6	6	3	1	5

The equations listed are all hidden in the grid. As you find them, draw a line through or circle around them. We've done these ones for you!

Equations can go up, down, diagonally, and backward.

You will also find a list of equations, like these:

7x10=70	2÷2=1	7x2=14
5x5=25	90÷10=9	30÷5=6

On some pages you will need to solve the problem before you look for the complete equation in the grid.

TOP TIPS!

The puzzles get harder toward the end of the book, so it's a good idea to start at the beginning and work your way through.

You'll find all the answers on pages 87-96. Try not to check them until you've finished the puzzle completely.

Remember, when equations are shown backward in the grid, double digit numbers are backward too! For instance, in this grid, the answer to "7x2" is read from right to left, giving the answer "14."

Let's get started with some number fun!

Superhero sums

Can you find all the equations from the one times table in this grid?

÷	4	9	1	2	x	1	=	1	2	÷	2	5	5	1
–	9	2	5	–	+	+	6	4	x	2	–	7	9	÷
+	6	0	=	6	7	2	0	x	9	1	7	6	2	3
x	÷	5	1	7	7	7	2	4	2	7	2	÷	÷	9
8	5	6	x	1	1	=	1	x	1	1	8	x	0	8
6	2	2	5	4	1	3	x	–	7	x	2	÷	7	2
3	=	1	x	3	0	1	=	1	x	0	1	6	–	x
2	8	6	–	8	2	3	2	4	5	8	9	2	9	+
8	3	4	–	4	÷	5	3	5	9	0	=	+	7	+
3	4	0	=	6	4	8	7	5	–	1	0	3	0	x
0	2	1	1	x	1	=	1	6	x	9	8	0	÷	4
1	x	–	–	2	1	–	x	2	4	x	9	÷	5	÷
4	+	5	5	x	8	1	5	4	1	1	0	8	0	2
0	1	5	7	1	=	9	0	=	6	=	6	+	2	3
5	8	9	3	6	÷	6	8	1	1	9	6	5	+	7

1x1=1
2x1=2
3x1=3
4x1=4

5x1=5
6x1=6
7x1=7
8x1=8

9x1=9
10x1=10
11x1=11
12x1=12

Wildlife wonders

Now let's try the two times table. Can you find the equations listed below?

6	+	0	6	+	3	8	3	7	6	7	3	2	+	4
9	3	9	1	x	2	=	2	=	8	3	x	2	=	6
9	9	1	=	4	x	4	9	2	x	4	1	3	2	6
0	5	x	2	=	1	0	+	3	÷	2	÷	÷	8	3
3	÷	+	–	+	3	2	5	7	–	=	+	9	4	+
x	8	+	1	4	x	=	2	2	0	2	7	9	4	2
9	3	1	2	0	6	2	1	0	x	x	7	3	x	2
6	x	3	8	0	4	x	–	9	6	2	8	1	÷	=
÷	8	4	4	4	+	0	–	1	÷	1	x	5	4	2
5	5	1	8	÷	2	1	8	0	5	7	2	2	=	x
+	0	=	=	9	÷	1	9	+	6	1	=	6	2	1
6	5	2	2	2	7	2	=	9	x	7	1	3	x	1
x	9	x	x	÷	x	4	3	2	+	÷	6	x	2	5
2	÷	7	4	6	3	9	=	5	x	9	x	6	3	+
9	7	–	3	+	6	2	–	5	6	6	3	6	x	3

1x2=2
2x2=4
3x2=6
4x2=8

5x2=10
6x2=12
7x2=14
8x2=16

9x2=18
10x2=20
11x2=22
12x2=24

Time to party

It's fun finding equations from the five times table! Can you look for them?

7	9	2	0	5	6	2	x	0	9	2	0	x	2	÷
3	8	x	5	=	4	0	6	2	x	÷	2	5	2	–
7	3	9	0	5	9	1	5	x	4	0	2	x	6	–
4	+	5	2	4	1	5	1	–	0	6	–	x	8	4
1	6	x	9	2	4	7	÷	x	8	8	5	6	4	2
x	÷	+	–	=	8	2	1	3	5	7	9	–	–	4
5	6	1	5	1	4	3	x	2	0	=	1	8	5	9
÷	1	x	8	4	8	8	+	0	x	4	5	5	0	7
5	9	=	3	1	7	2	3	+	1	5	2	5	6	5
2	6	7	5	x	4	3	9	0	2	7	=	5	8	6
=	+	0	5	x	8	4	2	x	–	5	2	6	+	1
5	4	=	7	0	3	2	5	9	x	÷	9	8	0	x
x	3	3	5	6	8	=	2	0	3	2	2	4	8	5
5	2	8	5	6	1	3	1	6	x	5	=	3	0	=
5	+	6	9	0	6	0	2	=	5	x	4	7	4	5

1x5=5
2x5=10
3x5=15
4x5=20

5x5=25
6x5=30
7x5=35
8x5=40

9x5=45
10x5=50
11x5=55
12x5=60

10x table

Arrr, me hearty!

How about trying the ten times table? All the equations are in the grid!

0	+	8	0	x	6	1	4	7	0	4	÷	1	8	9
6	7	9	3	3	2	6	7	5	4	7	–	0	8	–
+	1	=	–	6	=	3	=	8	7	0	–	9	2	8
6	6	0	0	6	x	0	1	1	=	0	1	x	1	1
6	5	4	5	1	1	1	1	7	1	x	6	1	2	6
–	2	+	1	x	x	3	0	x	8	1	4	+	0	–
3	x	1	5	2	2	7	9	=	3	7	4	8	9	9
4	1	1	4	÷	x	0	÷	x	6	+	9	3	=	1
2	0	5	2	2	6	1	8	x	1	0	=	8	0	+
–	=	1	9	6	8	=	0	3	6	3	2	7	1	5
9	2	6	3	5	7	0	0	=	1	3	÷	+	x	9
2	0	8	4	0	0	1	=	0	1	x	0	1	9	3
5	2	5	3	9	9	x	0	x	1	2	÷	5	9	0
x	7	6	4	3	x	1	3	4	x	1	0	=	4	0
8	x	7	–	1	–	3	1	2	+	1	0	5	5	4

1x10=10
2x10=20
3x10=30
4x10=40

5x10=50
6x10=60
7x10=70
8x10=80

9x10=90
10x10=100
11x10=110
12x10=120

Yeee ha!

It's time to round up some numbers! Remember, equations may be written backward in the grid.

4	8	6	7	÷	1	+	7	+	4	8	0	4	÷	7
2	7	6	–	x	8	3	÷	6	x	1	=	6	8	6
4	x	2	=	8	1	3	+	2	4	2	1	+	+	5
÷	0	1	9	1	3	0	4	3	8	0	5	7	2	x
x	5	1	0	9	5	3	=	7	x	5	=	3	5	6
+	6	0	9	x	0	6	7	7	5	6	3	4	0	–
+	0	x	2	3	2	0	9	5	0	–	6	3	x	3
0	2	1	+	7	3	=	=	7	÷	8	8	x	3	5
5	4	0	–	=	4	5	2	3	4	x	+	1	7	x
3	9	=	0	6	x	2	0	0	9	2	9	=	7	1
9	+	1	÷	1	5	5	0	1	x	=	3	3	4	=
7	x	0	1	0	=	0	7	7	9	1	4	1	4	5
3	6	0	2	1	2	8	0	4	5	6	4	2	8	6
8	7	2	2	÷	0	4	8	0	2	3	2	2	4	8
4	8	8	3	8	5	9	x	0	0	8	0	+	6	1

6x1=6
7x10=70
11x5=55
4x2=8

3x1=3
7x5=35
10x10=100
8x2=16

10x2=20
4x5=20
3x10=30
5x1=5

1, 2, 5, 10 times tables

Get ready to dive!

Dive down deep and discover the answers to these equations, then look for them in the grid.

x	5	5	9	7	0	0	6	+	1	6	5	9	0	x
1	0	0	5	6	9	0	4	7	=	x	9	8	4	0
–	0	5	2	=	1	x	2	2	+	4	0	1	5	8
5	x	1	0	=	5	0	x	8	1	=	2	x	9	+
÷	1	1	0	9	–	3	6	÷	9	5	9	5	1	4
4	÷	5	1	5	4	0	–	x	x	5	4	x	–	2
x	9	8	1	2	0	–	5	5	5	2	8	2	4	3
8	3	6	=	2	–	–	÷	9	5	=	x	=	8	0
9	–	÷	0	5	x	x	–	x	2	6	3	1	2	4
x	4	+	1	7	x	1	+	6	8	6	7	0	1	=
1	2	0	x	7	3	5	0	–	3	8	x	+	=	0
0	0	6	1	8	4	1	÷	=	1	0	5	8	1	1
=	4	8	1	0	1	–	2	x	1	–	2	6	x	x
9	3	7	5	2	=	5	x	5	x	2	0	4	2	4
0	+	4	5	3	+	0	1	5	0	9	0	2	1	2

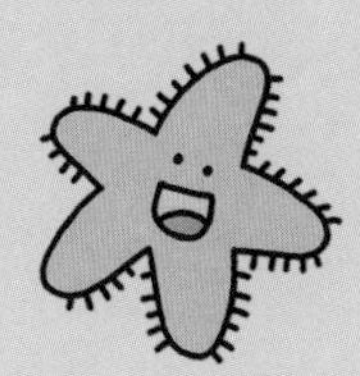

12x1=
3x2=
6x5=
9x10=

2x1=
5x2=
4x10=
5x5=

11x10=
5x10=
9x2=
12x10=

Dividing by 1

Dino dividing

Let's try some dividing now. Can you look for equations that divide by one?

3	÷	1	=	3	2	x	9	2	7	–	4	+	÷	0
x	4	–	–	8	÷	x	6	x	÷	8	–	4	8	1
4	8	3	4	+	1	8	2	x	0	3	÷	–	1	0
1	6	–	x	÷	=	÷	+	5	0	–	8	0	0	6
÷	2	3	4	6	2	3	=	÷	–	3	5	6	8	1
+	x	9	x	5	8	1	4	8	+	÷	5	8	8	7
8	÷	÷	4	–	÷	2	8	0	4	9	7	4	÷	+
8	5	8	2	5	1	6	0	3	2	1	8	–	1	–
8	0	5	1	=	+	6	1	8	6	÷	x	–	=	–
4	9	6	1	0	x	÷	5	0	0	1	2	9	8	4
–	2	÷	÷	6	1	6	0	5	÷	=	4	4	9	7
÷	2	6	8	4	3	÷	1	+	+	1	=	3	3	÷
1	1	÷	1	=	1	1	5	9	÷	1	=	9	1	1
x	2	1	x	6	9	=	9	5	÷	6	2	1	x	=
2	3	4	0	÷	x	6	5	4	5	4	2	÷	0	7

1÷1=1
2÷1=2
3÷1=3
4÷1=4

5÷1=5
6÷1=6
7÷1=7
8÷1=8

9÷1=9
10÷1=10
11÷1=11
12÷1=12

Dividing by 2

Socktastic!

Socks come in pairs. Can you find the equations that divide by two? Cross them off as you go.

÷	9	8	3	5	4	÷	6	9	3	6	÷	2	=	3
1	x	7	+	=	3	÷	3	1	4	–	0	6	2	÷
2	8	1	2	8	x	3	9	÷	4	1	x	0	4	5
÷	1	÷	1	0	4	+	3	7	=	÷	÷	9	+	x
2	8	7	2	9	+	0	x	2	4	÷	2	=	1	2
=	2	8	2	=	4	4	÷	7	–	–	0	=	8	x
6	2	+	3	4	9	0	4	5	1	5	1	÷	7	7
0	÷	5	2	0	2	5	9	x	8	0	8	+	0	÷
6	2	4	7	4	5	6	8	–	x	4	x	9	4	3
2	=	x	6	=	9	–	8	7	9	x	5	3	–	4
2	1	6	2	2	–	=	2	2	–	–	÷	3	–	9
÷	1	÷	=	+	2	3	2	÷	2	=	1	6	+	3
–	0	2	7	÷	4	7	–	–	8	4	5	8	–	8
1	÷	9	6	÷	3	1	7	8	x	6	3	1	0	0
4	9	1	÷	x	2	–	÷	4	9	6	8	9	5	0

2÷2=1
4÷2=2
6÷2=3
8÷2=4

10÷2=5
12÷2=6
14÷2=7
16÷2=8

18÷2=9
20÷2=10
22÷2=11
24÷2=12

Dividing by 5

Don't be scared!

Quick! Can you find the equations that divide by five, before the monsters do?

1	–	3	+	+	–	–	9	2	3	÷	1	3	x	0
0	1	8	x	4	4	5	0	÷	5	=	1	0	2	–
÷	1	+	–	3	1	5	6	0	3	7	2	8	5	8
5	7	4	1	–	+	4	9	1	7	6	÷	6	÷	4
=	0	6	1	+	4	3	4	=	2	9	=	7	5	x
2	4	–	9	1	5	+	5	0	7	5	3	4	=	0
–	3	x	8	–	÷	÷	2	0	÷	5	=	4	5	x
–	÷	+	+	4	5	–	4	0	x	5	+	7	2	÷
5	2	x	2	3	=	5	3	x	–	4	=	2	4	5
1	÷	1	x	3	9	1	5	÷	5	=	3	8	7	+
x	5	5	÷	5	=	1	1	9	1	2	8	4	9	1
x	5	÷	=	1	8	6	0	÷	5	=	1	2	6	–
x	7	x	4	1	2	÷	9	x	x	1	2	0	4	6
8	3	9	2	1	÷	x	7	9	5	x	2	3	0	3
2	0	0	8	4	4	5	6	3	+	2	0	x	8	x

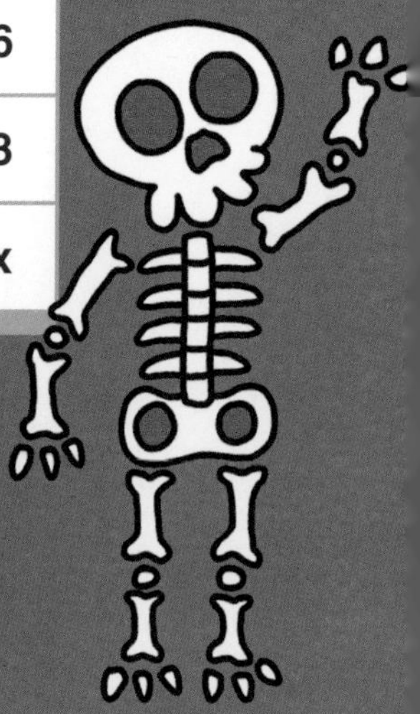

5÷5=1
10÷5=2
15÷5=3
20÷5=4

25÷5=5
30÷5=6
35÷5=7
40÷5=8

45÷5=9
50÷5=10
55÷5=11
60÷5=12

Dividing by 10

On safari

Wow! Look at all of the animals we can see.
Let's also spot the equations that divide by ten!

9	2	1	6	7	0	0	8	7	6	9	+	3	x	0
4	7	4	÷	0	9	8	5	=	÷	–	7	8	6	9
2	5	5	3	–	6	8	0	8	2	2	0	4	–	0
÷	3	4	+	1	5	1	4	÷	1	–	÷	x	5	÷
3	9	5	1	–	÷	=	1	3	1	6	1	5	0	1
+	5	+	–	0	0	3	5	0	÷	0	0	9	÷	0
1	4	8	6	1	6	4	1	–	÷	5	=	+	1	=
1	2	0	÷	1	0	=	1	2	1	1	7	8	0	9
7	7	0	6	0	0	8	7	+	1	–	0	–	=	3
÷	4	3	6	1	0	÷	1	0	=	1	5	=	5	+
8	3	0	÷	1	0	=	3	7	x	9	9	1	1	9
–	2	0	÷	1	0	=	2	8	÷	5	+	5	7	1
3	0	4	6	÷	7	x	5	0	9	5	–	1	–	6
1	x	–	4	3	+	6	5	–	5	÷	0	8	3	0
1	9	+	0	8	7	9	8	1	+	8	–	–	÷	1

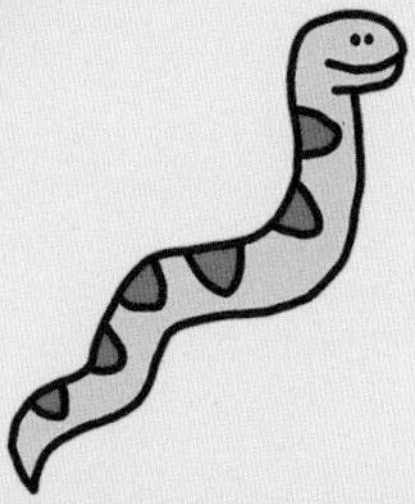

10÷10=1
20÷10=2
30÷10=3
40÷10=4

50÷10=5
60÷10=6
70÷10=7
80÷10=8

90÷10=9
100÷10=10
110÷10=11
120÷10=12

Dividing by 1, 2, 5, 10

Monster music

It's noisy at the monster band rehearsals.
Let's rehearse our divisions too!

1	6	1	5	2	+	9	÷	2	1	5	+	8	6	5
2	3	2	–	1	x	6	5	x	–	7	3	1	6	÷
0	6	6	9	8	3	=	0	–	2	0	÷	5	=	4
÷	5	8	7	9	1	3	8	–	4	9	2	x	1	5
1	6	8	+	÷	x	+	2	9	0	÷	4	5	3	3
0	x	7	5	0	÷	5	=	1	0	–	–	÷	9	0
=	9	8	+	4	9	8	1	2	8	8	9	9	x	3
1	2	0	÷	2	=	1	0	3	0	÷	5	=	6	3
2	2	2	=	0	=	+	x	9	4	6	8	6	3	0
1	6	1	1	5	2	5	5	2	÷	=	x	5	6	÷
+	÷	÷	÷	8	1	5	÷	8	1	9	7	1	2	1
2	0	5	÷	+	3	1	+	÷	9	5	÷	9	2	0
8	5	3	1	3	2	6	8	4	6	–	3	4	6	=
6	–	6	–	1	x	–	1	3	7	6	÷	8	9	3
2	4	÷	2	=	1	2	7	+	9	7	0	6	+	2

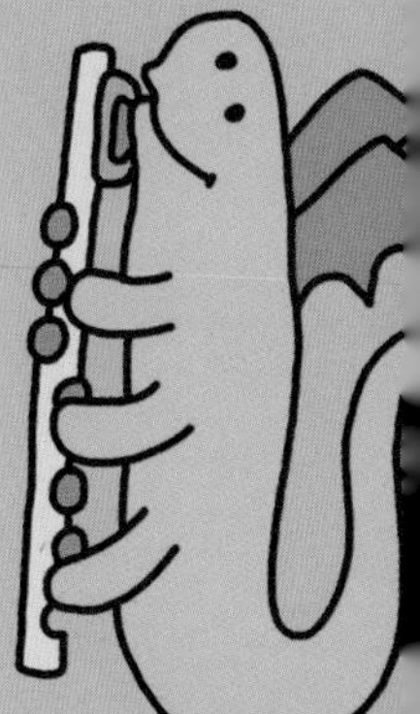

2÷1=2
80÷10=8
20÷5=4
20÷2=10

30÷5=6
24÷2=12
8÷1=8
5÷1=5

50÷5=10
30÷10=3
120÷10=12
55÷5=11

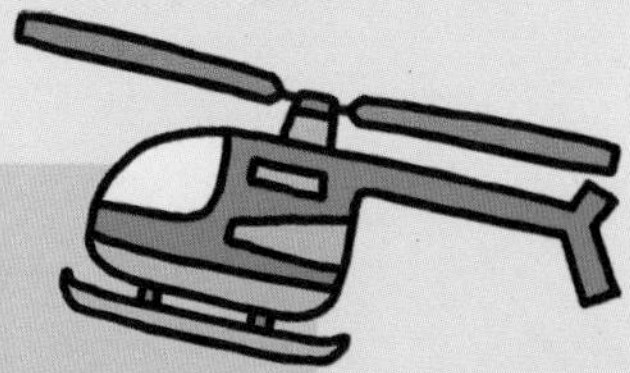

Dividing by 1, 2, 5, 10

Vrooom! We're off!

Let's get going with division! Complete the problem, then look for the equation in the grid.

1	+	−	5	+	0	+	6	+	−	6	3	7	9	3
4	5	5	0	2	5	÷	1	+	0	+	3	3	6	÷
+	0	+	0	2	0	+	0	0	−	4	4	6	x	x
x	3	−	−	÷	5	9	÷	+	7	5	−	÷	+	7
7	3	6	4	0	1	+	1	+	÷	÷	7	5	8	1
6	9	3	1	x	6	0	0	3	5	5	4	−	2	1
7	÷	4	3	5	÷	5	=	7	÷	=	+	6	9	0
4	1	1	÷	1	=	1	1	5	3	9	3	−	4	6
9	3	4	8	1	1	0	÷	1	0	=	1	1	2	÷
3	−	0	÷	x	2	x	1	2	2	6	x	9	8	4
7	5	÷	÷	2	+	÷	3	6	6	9	2	4	8	6
4	0	4	÷	0	=	8	2	1	9	8	9	−	÷	÷
1	0	÷	5	=	2	7	6	=	3	4	2	9	2	2
7	x	x	1	8	÷	2	=	9	6	8	8	6	=	=
x	7	0	+	7	1	7	5	1	8	4	−	−	4	3

35÷5=
6÷2=
45÷5=
50÷10=

11÷1=
14÷2=
12÷2=
18÷2=

8÷2=
110÷10=
10÷5=
10÷10=

Fun on the farm

It's time to try the three times table. Can you find the equations in the grid below?

7	x	3	=	2	1	8	1	4	0	6	0	6	7	1
3	8	1	÷	0	0	6	2	2	4	x	3	=	1	2
9	÷	5	3	4	2	0	9	+	6	x	÷	5	2	9
+	x	3	÷	1	1	–	0	=	3	1	4	x	x	4
7	1	4	7	1	6	3	3	=	÷	8	÷	–	3	2
x	7	3	9	x	=	x	9	–	4	9	0	8	=	7
7	+	6	2	3	2	x	x	2	x	1	8	÷	3	+
÷	3	1	x	=	3	3	=	3	0	–	1	÷	6	1
4	3	0	2	3	–	3	=	+	x	÷	=	3	÷	x
2	1	–	÷	3	x	2	3	3	x	8	3	7	9	4
9	3	2	÷	8	7	÷	+	9	x	x	x	x	x	÷
9	9	9	–	2	8	2	3	4	5	1	6	5	3	7
7	5	7	9	8	4	4	x	9	5	9	+	+	0	–
÷	8	+	4	+	9	–	5	3	3	5	6	5	4	2
2	–	5	5	1	=	3	x	5	6	+	1	+	1	4

1x3=3
2x3=6
3x3=9
4x3=12

5x3=15
6x3=18
7x3=21
8x3=24

9x3=27
10x3=30
11x3=33
12x3=36

It's all blue!

Don't be blue! The four times table is lots of fun– as you will see when you find the equations below.

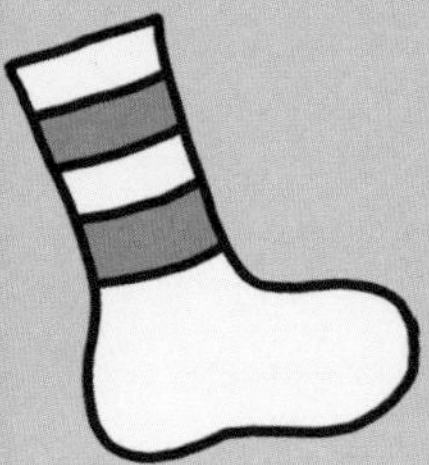

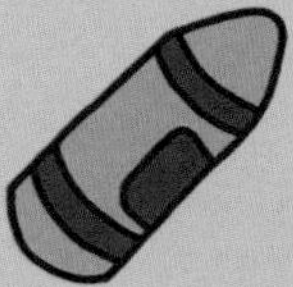

1	5	4	x	+	2	5	4	2	x	0	4	3	2	7
3	0	8	÷	4	7	4	1	2	x	4	=	4	8	8
6	0	x	2	1	=	4	x	3	=	1	7	5	4	+
÷	x	2	4	1	6	1	5	4	x	2	–	9	÷	x
5	9	5	x	=	4	8	x	4	9	x	4	=	3	6
÷	3	4	x	9	4	1	9	÷	–	4	5	7	4	8
–	=	9	+	4	1	0	3	x	x	–	3	2	7	9
4	+	6	2	8	=	+	–	4	–	7	=	–	x	8
6	6	1	1	4	2	2	=	x	÷	4	÷	–	4	6
x	4	3	x	8	8	1	0	–	x	3	2	+	=	4
÷	6	2	3	÷	6	7	x	6	1	–	3	x	2	7
x	7	x	÷	–	x	9	0	9	9	6	=	2	8	2
6	2	4	–	7	1	9	7	2	4	8	4	4	x	3
3	3	=	+	8	+	4	0	1	7	7	x	x	÷	2
9	1	8	0	3	5	–	x	1	–	5	8	1	3	7

1x4=4
2x4=8
3x4=12
4x4=16
5x4=20
6x4=24
7x4=28
8x4=32
9x4=36
10x4=40
11x4=44
12x4=48

Creation station

Can you find equations from the three and four times tables here?

9	7	x	4	x	0	6	x	x	2	7	2	1	8	0
2	0	1	6	5	1	0	4	÷	9	6	5	1	4	6
7	3	0	8	x	4	=	3	2	1	9	3	6	1	3
0	6	1	3	4	4	8	8	–	3	6	3	1	x	3
x	x	=	6	0	–	4	2	8	2	2	2	3	2	÷
÷	3	8	x	3	=	2	4	x	+	x	=	x	3	7
0	=	1	+	x	3	x	÷	8	4	9	x	3	+	2
3	1	2	÷	4	6	3	–	=	1	9	–	5	4	7
=	8	x	4	=	6	0	4	4	–	0	x	1	x	+
3	6	3	4	1	1	8	3	5	5	÷	+	7	6	8
x	7	=	=	2	5	–	1	6	3	1	4	7	5	5
0	7	3	4	3	2	8	÷	0	4	=	4	x	0	1
1	1	6	x	x	7	8	6	x	7	7	2	9	2	7
9	–	0	1	7	–	2	4	0	2	=	4	x	5	5
–	1	x	1	0	x	2	4	6	9	7	8	3	x	8

8x3=24
8x4=32
10x3=30
5x4=20

6x3=18
11x4=44
1x3=3
12x4=48

3x3=9
10x4=40
12x3=36
3x4=12

Animal antics

Time for some jungle number fun. Complete these equations using the three and four times tables.

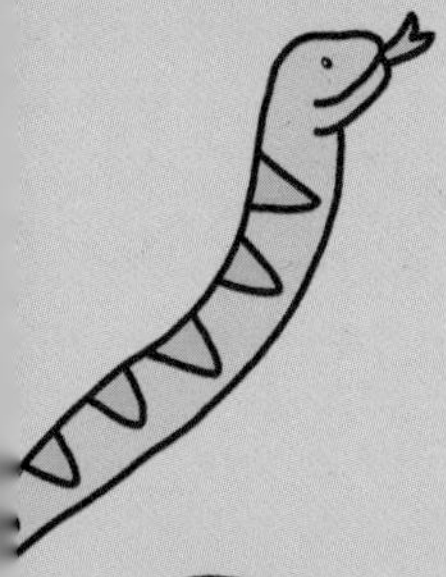

9	−	+	0	7	x	6	+	4	2	=	4	x	6	8
5	4	−	6	6	4	4	5	0	2	6	+	÷	4	4
4	4	x	3	=	1	2	+	3	3	0	2	−	6	+
3	3	=	3	x	1	1	8	=	0	3	8	+	9	÷
1	3	3	÷	7	1	6	4	2	9	−	x	1	x	7
2	4	9	8	5	÷	x	5	9	=	1	2	x	3	÷
=	5	5	x	8	9	9	1	9	3	4	5	6	=	+
3	3	1	8	5	9	8	=	÷	−	5	x	7	2	x
x	−	−	÷	=	0	8	3	5	÷	3	9	7	7	7
7	8	4	0	+	4	4	x	4	7	6	÷	4	−	0
÷	3	4	=	5	3	x	5	5	6	7	1	÷	6	4
0	8	÷	6	4	2	4	2	2	=	1	x	4	6	2
x	7	2	8	5	x	=	+	9	3	+	0	÷	÷	−
x	9	7	÷	5	÷	1	4	9	x	+	7	6	−	0
8	−	+	2	+	2	6	9	9	2	9	+	4	0	+

4x4=
5x3=
2x4=
4x3=

7x4=
11x3=
6x4=
7x3=

1x4=
9x3=
9x4=
2x3=

Little critters

Now let's try dividing by three. Have a look at the equations and then find them in the grid.

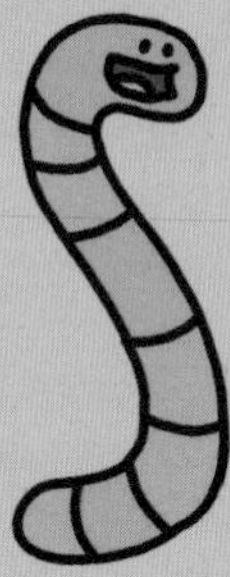

1	x	8	5	x	÷	9	–	1	+	6	4	0	1	4
0	+	–	3	x	7	6	8	7	7	4	–	9	2	–
6	–	8	4	÷	÷	6	x	x	1	2	4	0	÷	x
3	÷	8	9	9	4	+	9	1	1	+	8	7	3	5
7	9	6	3	0	–	0	1	=	5	6	2	8	=	4
7	1	÷	÷	÷	+	=	3	4	2	1	9	÷	4	9
6	3	3	4	8	3	÷	1	1	1	9	x	5	0	÷
1	8	=	2	÷	3	9	=	÷	1	5	÷	3	=	5
6	5	2	3	0	÷	3	=	1	0	8	6	÷	7	2
1	0	3	8	2	÷	8	5	0	÷	3	6	2	2	0
8	5	5	5	6	1	3	5	9	÷	9	0	3	7	5
÷	0	4	3	x	7	÷	1	4	x	3	2	÷	÷	+
3	3	+	6	4	2	8	3	+	0	3	7	8	3	7
=	÷	6	3	9	5	+	x	=	2	4	÷	3	=	8
6	+	x	0	9	÷	3	=	3	7	0	8	0	9	3

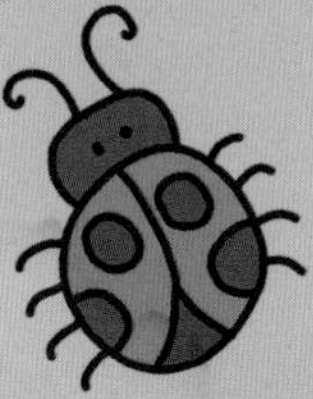
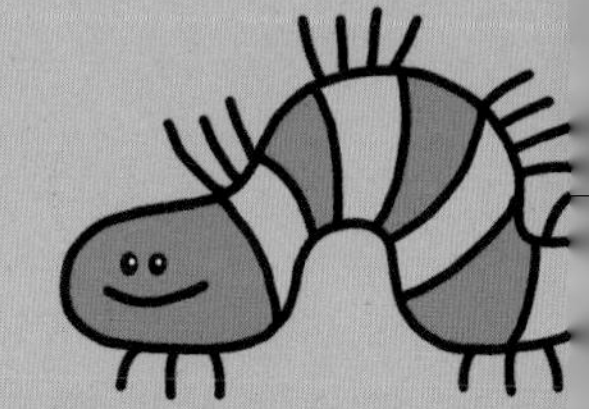

3÷3=1
6÷3=2
9÷3=3
12÷3=4

15÷3=5
18÷3=6
21÷3=7
24÷3=8

27÷3=9
30÷3=10
33÷3=11
36÷3=12

Dividing by 4

In the team

Each equation you find is a point for your team.
Find them all and you've won the game!

6	3	3	–	1	+	1	x	–	4	9	8	5	4	0
1	4	–	4	4	7	–	8	5	x	1	+	7	–	3
2	0	4	4	9	1	x	0	0	9	1	0	4	5	2
÷	÷	1	x	÷	9	1	2	=	÷	6	4	6	+	÷
4	4	3	6	–	9	0	4	÷	8	÷	8	5	x	4
=	=	7	÷	8	8	÷	3	1	–	4	÷	–	2	=
3	1	0	1	0	6	+	4	9	2	=	4	4	0	8
5	0	9	1	3	8	4	+	1	6	4	=	4	÷	+
x	+	6	+	+	6	8	2	4	3	0	1	÷	4	2
3	+	5	7	2	x	7	6	÷	÷	x	2	4	=	–
1	9	9	=	6	+	5	4	x	6	4	9	=	5	8
x	÷	4	x	1	+	÷	8	5	5	x	=	1	x	x
5	÷	8	6	2	8	8	9	x	7	1	5	1	9	4
8	+	9	4	–	3	0	3	7	4	7	+	2	7	x
2	8	÷	4	=	7	2	4	÷	4	=	6	7	5	0

4÷4=1
8÷4=2
12÷4=3
16÷4=4

20÷4=5
24÷4=6
28÷4=7
32÷4=8

36÷4=9
40÷4=10
44÷4=11
48÷4=12

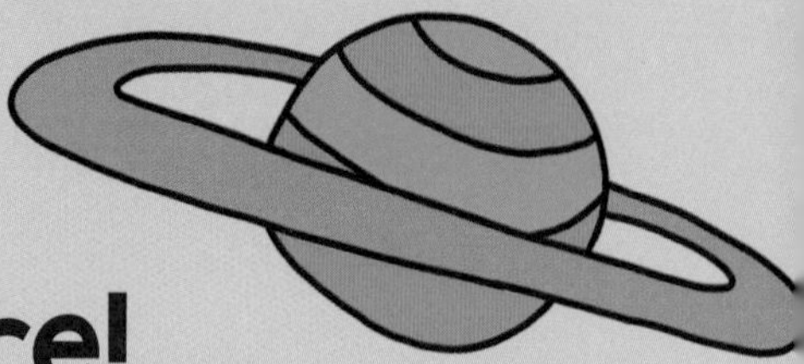

Equations are out there!

Look out for aliens as you find the equations using three and four!

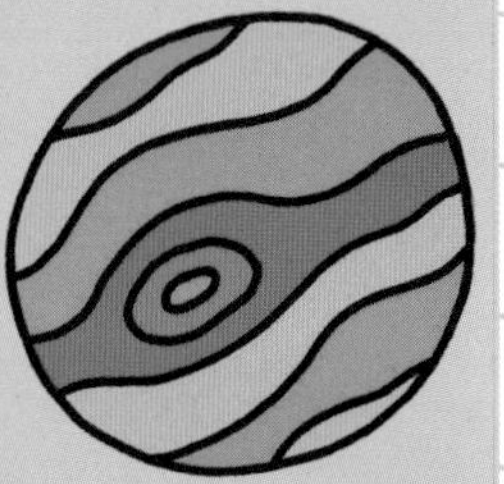

1	2	÷	4	=	3	6	5	5	7	3	9	3	1	+
0	6	2	4	2	2	–	–	6	÷	x	4	+	8	8
2	+	6	5	3	÷	4	6	5	0	x	–	÷	÷	–
8	÷	4	=	2	6	=	÷	+	2	3	+	x	3	1
3	8	1	–	0	4	4	1	3	+	4	4	9	=	7
9	x	5	0	÷	7	1	8	9	=	6	÷	1	6	1
8	2	6	4	1	=	=	8	+	6	8	4	4	÷	÷
x	x	2	x	4	4	7	5	3	+	6	–	9	=	2
6	7	9	÷	÷	5	x	2	x	x	4	5	3	8	1
–	÷	4	2	7	4	÷	7	4	7	–	+	0	1	÷
4	4	3	–	3	–	6	7	5	+	2	4	÷	4	3
9	6	0	=	7	8	4	7	x	÷	0	1	3	6	=
5	2	7	6	2	1	6	4	8	9	6	÷	=	4	7
+	7	0	9	÷	3	=	3	4	2	4	3	1	÷	2
7	5	7	9	3	8	0	9	x	8	5	÷	0	x	8

18÷3=6
12÷4=3
24÷3=8
44÷4=11

9÷3=3
32÷4=8
30÷3=10
4÷4=1

6÷3=2
24÷4=6
21÷3=7
8÷4=2

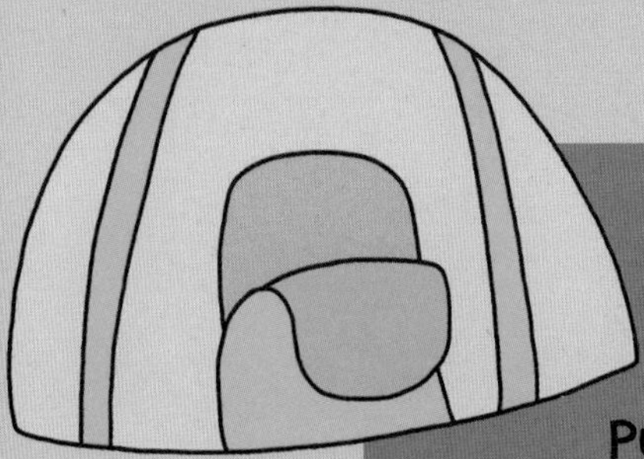

Dividing by 3 and 4

Let's go camping

Put up your tent, then find the equations and answers in the grid.

7	3	÷	8	–	1	2	8	÷	4	=	7	1	8	2
7	4	8	÷	4	=	1	2	2	x	÷	4	6	5	5
9	0	0	9	x	5	4	7	7	1	0	8	÷	6	0
5	4	2	3	=	6	0	0	1	–	–	6	4	3	1
x	+	2	4	8	1	5	7	÷	6	2	x	=	÷	+
–	+	÷	3	x	–	9	x	5	4	6	2	4	3	4
4	0	6	+	7	–	3	0	6	÷	=	9	1	=	–
2	1	0	3	2	8	x	6	1	3	–	1	8	1	9
7	7	2	6	3	9	5	6	÷	2	1	2	0	=	1
7	9	5	6	=	÷	0	9	1	3	6	÷	4	5	2
1	x	+	3	6	1	3	4	8	÷	=	÷	4	÷	÷
÷	7	÷	–	9	–	9	=	7	5	6	1	7	÷	3
5	7	1	5	÷	3	=	5	1	3	+	7	2	÷	=
2	0	3	–	–	9	÷	4	1	1	+	–	7	+	4
6	9	2	7	+	7	x	4	6	2	9	8	4	+	3

28÷4=
36÷3=
48÷4=
33÷3=

36÷4=
3÷3=
40÷4=
15÷3=

20÷4=
27÷3=
16÷4=
12÷3=

Robot runabout

Beep! Beep! The robots are keen to learn the six times table. Can you help them?

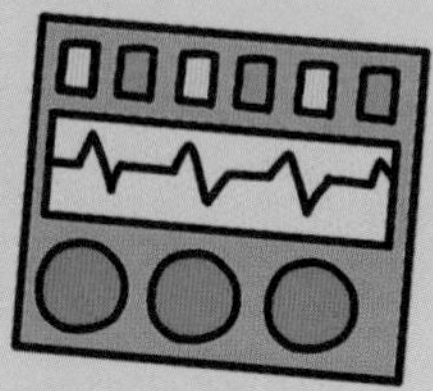

8	0	+	7	–	8	7	0	3	=	6	x	5	–	2
÷	7	7	4	4	1	0	8	2	3	2	8	5	4	8
6	0	–	7	4	2	1	4	–	7	0	x	0	2	1
7	8	+	+	2	8	1	=	+	9	=	x	0	6	3
9	4	–	3	0	0	x	6	1	7	3	6	–	÷	9
5	x	0	5	4	8	6	x	2	3	7	÷	x	÷	x
6	6	–	9	7	÷	=	8	5	÷	5	9	1	2	2
4	=	3	8	1	9	6	7	8	1	4	1	8	2	1
÷	2	3	–	x	1	6	9	2	3	3	1	0	1	7
0	4	÷	6	0	3	2	–	–	3	–	0	9	=	2
2	0	=	+	=	x	1	1	4	x	0	x	5	6	4
÷	5	÷	6	8	2	x	9	6	8	2	6	–	x	=
4	÷	x	8	1	=	6	x	3	1	4	=	0	2	6
6	6	5	0	x	÷	=	7	0	1	7	6	1	–	x
6	4	8	6	x	8	6	3	÷	÷	7	0	7	0	7

1x6=6
2x6=12
3x6=18
4x6=24

5x6=30
6x6=36
7x6=42
8x6=48

9x6=54
10x6=60
11x6=66
12x6=72

Tournament time

Find the equations in the seven times table to help the knights wake up the king!

2	2	1	0	2	–	5	9	2	4	1	5	1	8	1
9	7	+	+	4	1	+	–	6	1	3	3	4	6	2
8	+	÷	2	=	4	5	8	x	8	6	x	3	1	x
1	4	+	5	7	x	1	7	6	6	=	7	9	5	7
0	7	5	7	x	8	=	4	5	1	7	=	6	x	=
x	0	÷	–	6	7	5	=	8	6	x	2	2	+	8
7	9	4	2	7	1	7	0	7	+	9	1	+	2	4
=	1	4	0	7	x	8	2	x	7	=	1	4	6	5
7	4	2	0	8	9	4	=	7	x	7	9	8	5	0
0	÷	÷	+	4	1	5	9	0	7	2	0	2	x	4
7	+	÷	x	8	6	–	1	–	0	5	1	=	7	9
8	3	x	9	+	–	7	x	÷	0	4	3	7	=	1
2	3	0	8	9	6	1	7	0	4	6	4	x	3	3
7	9	7	4	–	8	7	=	8	3	4	6	4	5	9
3	2	2	1	5	÷	x	7	x	÷	1	–	9	2	6

1x7=7
2x7=14
3x7=21
4x7=28

5x7=35
6x7=42
7x7=49
8x7=56

9x7=63
10x7=70
11x7=77
12x7=84

Bird spotting

There are lots of birds about today. Can you find some equations too?

2	0	6	=	6	x	0	1	5	2	9	8	÷	8	6
0	–	2	7	=	6	x	2	1	0	–	7	2	x	4
–	4	+	2	5	6	8	2	4	+	4	4	x	+	2
5	5	3	6	–	÷	7	3	9	x	1	8	1	–	÷
1	8	–	9	÷	4	1	1	x	1	6	–	x	3	x
÷	4	4	8	=	7	x	2	1	6	2	6	x	6	1
6	3	=	6	x	6	+	x	6	5	=	7	0	0	5
3	5	2	8	7	+	8	0	1	6	3	1	x	1	3
x	7	3	1	7	÷	2	2	6	2	3	9	8	3	–
7	x	9	7	=	9	+	6	6	=	6	x	1	2	0
=	6	6	4	7	÷	2	–	x	5	3	+	5	9	0
2	=	3	÷	x	+	÷	x	8	0	=	1	4	0	7
1	4	2	0	1	1	x	÷	3	4	x	7	=	2	8
2	2	8	6	1	2	x	–	3	9	5	3	x	6	÷
0	7	=	7	x	0	1	1	–	1	8	+	x	8	2

10x6=60
4x7=28
6x6=36
11x7=77

12x6=72
10x7=70
1x6=6
8x7=56

7x6=42
12x7=84
3x6=18
3x7=21

In the sunshine

It's a lovely day for sitting outside and finding equations from the six and seven times tables.

x	5	3	1	1	6	–	5	5	+	8	÷	÷	÷	4
1	1	x	6	=	6	6	+	8	0	8	7	0	x	÷
7	=	7	x	1	9	x	6	=	5	4	3	6	x	–
8	0	÷	1	9	5	+	–	5	1	6	=	7	3	4
3	7	3	6	–	7	2	+	5	9	2	6	9	–	4
–	8	6	8	–	8	0	x	5	4	7	2	8	+	9
x	4	1	9	4	3	4	4	3	+	6	÷	0	7	4
x	9	8	8	x	5	–	=	0	÷	2	÷	3	6	=
4	1	5	4	–	x	3	8	6	÷	9	4	=	2	7
2	2	1	÷	4	4	1	=	7	x	2	8	6	÷	x
1	2	4	=	7	x	6	9	7	8	8	7	x	+	7
=	–	3	6	7	–	–	1	+	x	3	5	5	2	7
6	3	6	x	9	–	÷	+	5	1	5	2	7	0	5
x	7	+	8	1	2	4	9	9	0	0	5	x	7	x
2	9	x	7	=	6	3	÷	0	6	5	6	4	8	4

2x7=
8x6=
6x7=
4x6=

5x7=
2x6=
1x7=
9x6=

9x7=
11x6=
7x7=
5x6=

Dividing by 6

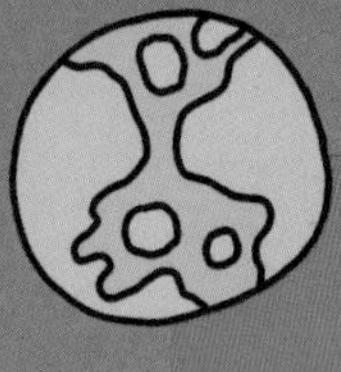

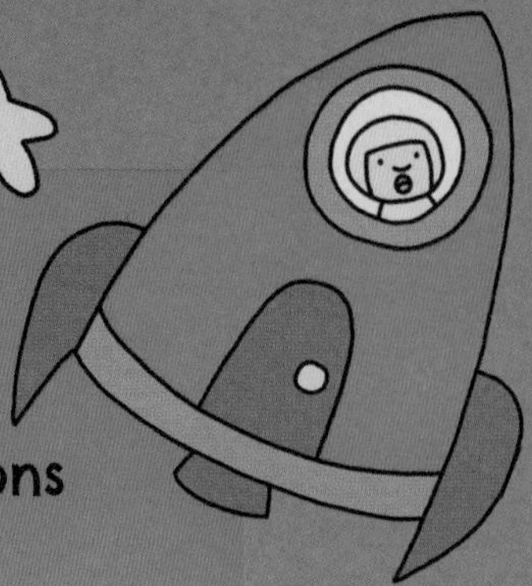

Time for takeoff!

Let's try dividing by six. Can you find the equations in the grid below?

–	9	–	x	6	1	–	3	2	8	8	1	2	–	x
–	+	5	8	0	3	1	1	–	1	=	2	4	x	3
6	+	0	7	5	0	4	8	÷	6	=	8	÷	4	6
2	7	6	9	4	4	5	5	÷	8	0	0	6	–	÷
0	1	3	1	7	0	2	6	3	3	x	4	=	6	6
7	0	–	x	2	5	÷	0	6	x	x	1	4	7	=
3	1	7	2	x	÷	8	÷	7	÷	7	2	x	2	6
5	2	x	1	÷	7	6	6	÷	1	6	3	4	÷	–
5	3	3	8	3	8	4	=	6	x	3	=	8	6	8
2	0	÷	÷	2	–	5	1	2	9	1	1	1	=	3
3	8	1	6	7	+	4	0	–	1	8	–	5	1	+
–	9	9	=	0	5	÷	9	5	7	0	5	1	2	9
0	7	6	3	2	8	6	2	1	4	2	÷	6	=	7
3	x	–	+	2	÷	=	+	8	6	÷	3	–	7	7
3	0	÷	6	=	5	9	+	3	1	6	3	5	÷	–

6÷6=1
12÷6=2
18÷6=3
24÷6=4

30÷6=5
36÷6=6
42÷6=7
48÷6=8

54÷6=9
60÷6=10
66÷6=11
72÷6=12

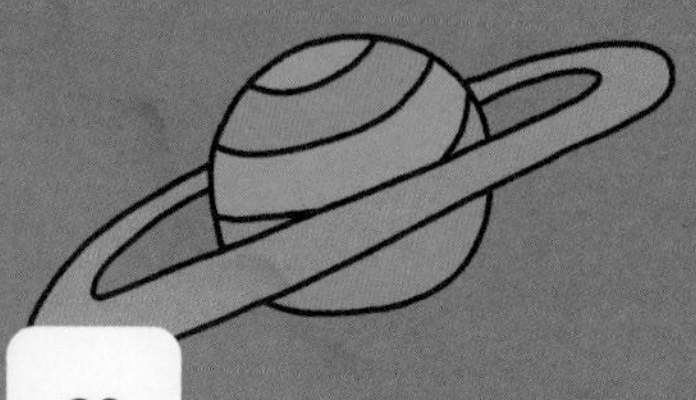

Number heroes!

Are you ready for a daring rescue? We need to divide by seven and you're the hero!

x	3	÷	9	6	1	5	2	x	+	5	7	7	9	0
4	4	0	2	=	3	÷	2	6	–	3	6	9	9	8
2	1	÷	7	=	3	4	9	÷	7	=	7	–	2	7
–	7	÷	+	8	4	4	÷	7	1	–	6	6	3	5
8	7	1	+	1	4	x	2	0	7	4	7	5	0	7
9	÷	3	÷	1	–	÷	5	÷	7	4	÷	0	2	3
–	7	÷	4	6	2	=	7	7	7	6	5	7	8	2
6	=	x	4	7	7	0	0	=	5	=	8	3	=	–
3	1	9	4	÷	1	÷	6	1	1	1	6	2	0	2
÷	1	6	5	9	9	7	2	0	6	2	+	4	3	4
7	3	3	8	1	9	5	6	÷	7	=	8	÷	+	–
=	+	5	2	+	÷	1	9	+	5	4	–	1	8	7
9	8	+	3	7	4	2	8	÷	7	=	4	7	5	3
4	3	–	9	4	2	8	÷	1	4	9	0	3	+	+
9	7	4	4	7	÷	7	2	0	5	9	1	8	4	÷

7÷7=1
14÷7=2
21÷7=3
28÷7=4

35÷7=5
42÷7=6
49÷7=7
56÷7=8

63÷7=9
70÷7=10
77÷7=11
84÷7=12

It's a wild life!

Look around for wild animals and equations. Can you find them all?

3	7	÷	9	÷	5	5	0	8	5	3	2	+	0	9
6	0	1	0	0	1	2	÷	6	=	2	1	+	+	9
÷	3	÷	÷	5	5	–	3	7	0	8	1	1	5	7
6	7	7	6	0	0	6	+	5	0	3	7	x	4	0
=	6	3	7	=	÷	3	÷	0	9	9	6	8	1	÷
6	1	8	4	x	5	8	1	4	2	x	–	6	x	7
+	4	÷	9	7	9	=	1	4	÷	7	=	2	4	=
3	x	6	4	=	6	9	1	4	6	1	1	x	8	1
4	6	–	7	÷	2	1	x	4	=	9	2	x	x	0
7	0	÷	0	7	x	4	=	7	+	9	1	4	5	÷
7	3	6	–	8	0	6	÷	1	3	3	÷	–	÷	÷
6	1	–	2	8	÷	7	=	4	4	9	÷	7	=	7
+	8	+	+	4	2	÷	6	=	7	4	0	6	5	7
÷	4	5	2	3	5	5	8	0	÷	+	6	0	9	3
6	3	+	6	+	÷	9	8	5	1	3	+	1	7	8

36÷6=6
49÷7=7
42÷6=7
14÷7=2

60÷6=10
70÷7=10
24÷6=4
7÷7=1

30÷6=5
63÷7=9
12÷6=2
28÷7=4

Birthday bash

Get ready for a party by finding the equations in the list, and their answers.

6	8	4	÷	7	=	1	2	x	3	6	0	4	2	1
6	x	3	7	6	÷	5	7	–	2	x	7	3	–	8
÷	1	5	2	÷	x	÷	+	6	1	x	2	3	+	÷
6	8	3	6	7	+	7	5	0	÷	x	÷	4	5	5
=	÷	+	1	÷	4	5	4	1	9	+	6	–	2	–
1	6	8	–	3	7	8	1	9	2	4	=	7	÷	+
1	=	÷	6	0	x	=	=	7	8	x	1	5	8	8
–	3	4	4	0	7	6	8	–	7	4	2	+	3	5
4	3	÷	3	÷	÷	0	x	5	+	4	9	8	=	3
2	7	9	7	4	+	x	9	÷	9	+	4	7	2	0
÷	7	7	5	1	5	6	6	3	÷	6	÷	8	1	7
7	5	–	=	1	6	1	9	1	2	5	x	+	6	7
=	8	6	4	8	÷	6	=	8	3	3	x	+	0	9
6	÷	8	4	–	5	÷	÷	2	÷	7	x	9	2	1
6	5	1	6	–	0	6	2	1	÷	7	=	3	7	7

42÷7=
72÷6=
56÷7=
18÷6=

84÷7=
6÷6=
35÷7=
66÷6=

21÷7=
54÷6=
77÷7=
48÷6=

Treasure hunting

Find all the equations from the nine times table to help the pirates find the treasure.

4	0	8	0	1	0	9	0	1	8	2	0	4	9	7
+	0	=	−	7	3	5	÷	2	9	−	5	8	x	8
2	5	8	7	4	7	9	2	x	6	3	4	3	6	9
9	6	x	0	0	7	6	4	9	8	5	−	5	5	9
2	8	1	0	2	x	8	4	1	9	3	=	x	8	8
3	6	8	9	8	6	−	3	5	−	÷	8	8	−	+
=	+	3	=	+	3	5	8	2	1	=	−	5	x	9
8	3	4	1	6	1	4	5	8	4	2	6	÷	3	7
x	8	0	1	9	3	6	÷	0	8	=	8	x	0	1
4	2	+	2	=	8	=	0	6	4	7	+	2	+	1
6	7	÷	5	8	3	8	6	5	3	9	÷	5	5	9
4	=	5	4	x	3	x	8	=	2	4	4	9	−	7
8	8	x	4	2	2	8	0	7	÷	3	7	8	9	2
4	x	+	3	1	8	2	x	8	=	1	6	0	6	1
x	9	+	6	9	9	8	8	=	8	x	1	1	5	+

1x8=8
2x8=16
3x8=24
4x8=32
5x8=40
6x8=48
7x8=56
8x8=64
9x8=72
10x8=80
11x8=88
12x8=96

Wild West world

It's time to take a wild ride through the nine times table. Saddle up and find these equations!

x	1	0	x	9	=	9	0	0	3	x	2	2	9	1
2	2	÷	0	5	÷	5	–	8	9	4	9	0	÷	8
6	÷	–	2	1	9	7	3	3	7	7	–	7	6	0
6	1	5	4	=	9	x	5	1	6	1	6	7	1	1
x	4	4	9	2	+	+	÷	1	7	÷	8	3	5	=
9	–	+	8	8	7	8	8	4	7	8	1	2	9	9
3	7	+	7	3	6	=	7	7	1	–	1	5	9	x
–	x	6	2	3	9	4	9	÷	–	7	x	4	2	2
8	9	8	x	x	9	5	4	x	2	1	4	6	2	1
9	=	2	9	+	+	=	x	=	8	9	5	1	0	5
8	6	1	=	8	6	9	9	–	1	8	x	–	3	3
1	3	x	1	3	6	x	=	9	9	=	9	x	1	1
÷	7	9	8	+	3	6	3	7	–	2	2	9	3	÷
1	÷	=	5	4	–	2	6	x	2	÷	0	9	3	3
7	+	9	6	1	3	7	5	0	7	6	6	+	9	–

1x9=9
2x9=18
3x9=27
4x9=36

5x9=45
6x9=54
7x9=63
8x9=72

9x9=81
10x9=90
11x9=99
12x9=108

8 and 9 times tables

The ocean deep

Many amazing animals live in the ocean. Look out for the eight and nine times tables as you swim.

0	0	0	÷	4	x	9	=	3	6	0	6	6	6	–
5	5	x	÷	1	9	÷	9	8	+	2	9	5	3	3
0	1	1	x	8	=	8	8	6	x	=	3	x	7	+
1	0	÷	2	–	÷	1	3	3	8	x	÷	8	1	8
0	–	x	+	9	4	2	5	x	9	5	+	=	2	3
x	8	–	5	x	9	2	2	=	2	3	2	4	3	4
9	9	8	5	7	0	1	2	9	8	3	0	0	7	7
=	3	5	7	4	9	7	x	4	9	9	=	8	7	x
9	6	6	3	5	÷	1	8	÷	6	=	5	8	x	7
0	÷	1	8	÷	x	7	=	÷	8	=	9	4	x	5
9	4	7	1	4	7	x	1	0	5	7	8	x	x	4
x	6	7	=	1	–	5	6	x	3	3	1	x	1	4
8	7	x	9	9	0	9	5	2	9	1	4	4	8	1
÷	x	3	x	6	÷	4	x	x	0	=	0	0	1	÷
3	–	2	2	÷	9	–	+	5	–	1	9	5	÷	2

12x8=96
4x9=36
5x8=40
10x9=90

11x8=88
1x9=9
4x8=32
3x9=27

2x8=16
11x9=99
8x8=64
2x9=18

Ancient giants

The dinosaurs are coming! Find all the equations in the list to stop them in their tracks!

4	x	÷	9	x	÷	2	÷	+	9	9	3	2	6	8
6	6	5	x	6	–	1	9	–	x	÷	x	0	5	–
8	÷	9	9	5	x	9	=	4	5	÷	7	1	0	÷
x	+	+	=	9	÷	3	7	+	3	+	3	6	6	0
–	x	5	8	÷	–	x	x	4	2	=	8	x	3	8
2	–	÷	1	3	2	6	x	÷	8	9	÷	÷	9	=
4	4	÷	+	8	6	9	+	x	8	4	3	x	x	8
7	x	0	÷	0	8	x	9	=	7	2	=	÷	7	x
0	1	3	0	1	7	5	3	6	2	5	8	8	5	0
4	–	÷	÷	=	x	7	÷	5	x	0	–	+	x	1
1	0	2	6	9	9	1	x	6	x	9	=	5	4	6
x	x	4	2	x	=	7	1	8	3	8	+	5	8	3
8	8	÷	+	2	6	4	x	8	=	3	2	1	3	8
=	2	0	÷	1	3	6	1	1	6	5	6	–	÷	0
8	8	9	2	9	x	4	–	3	0	+	6	2	3	6

9x9=
6x8=
5x9=
3x8=

12x9=
1x8=
8x9=
4x8=

7x9=
10x8=
6x9=
7x8=

Dividing by 8

It's a bug's life

What a lot of tiny creatures! Can you help them find the equations that divide by eight?

1	6	÷	8	=	2	9	8	8	1	+	9	7	8	÷
3	9	3	9	4	5	9	7	=	÷	÷	x	6	8	1
4	2	3	3	2	9	3	8	8	÷	8	=	1	1	+
5	1	÷	4	7	+	÷	+	5	8	3	+	–	4	1
9	6	6	8	1	8	x	5	0	9	0	7	6	0	8
6	4	÷	7	=	5	÷	+	9	x	9	8	7	=	8
÷	0	8	8	6	4	x	6	6	4	1	0	8	4	4
8	÷	7	3	=	3	5	4	÷	÷	7	÷	1	8	3
=	8	3	1	=	7	8	x	+	÷	4	8	2	÷	9
1	=	4	8	+	–	5	4	5	6	+	=	–	8	8
2	5	÷	9	7	2	÷	8	=	9	1	1	8	=	1
÷	4	5	5	÷	7	7	5	+	2	3	0	8	6	x
2	8	0	4	7	7	4	6	x	9	6	x	2	x	+
1	0	5	7	3	7	–	÷	4	5	9	x	÷	8	6
4	1	0	0	2	2	x	+	÷	÷	+	+	8	8	5

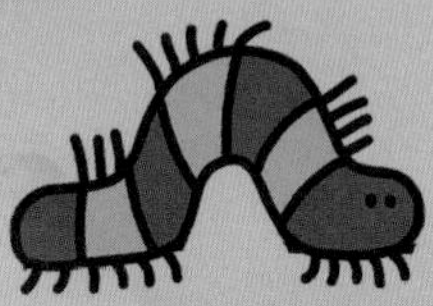

8÷8=1
16÷8=2
24÷8=3
32÷8=4

40÷8=5
48÷8=6
56÷8=7
64÷8=8

72÷8=9
80÷8=10
88÷8=11
96÷8=12

Dividing by 9

Haunted house

Help the ghosts divide by nine. Remember, equations may be written backward in the grid.

2	–	8	–	6	–	4	3	1	x	0	÷	0	5	x
7	7	÷	9	0	4	–	1	8	÷	9	=	2	÷	3
÷	4	9	4	9	3	=	1	5	6	3	÷	9	=	7
9	3	–	+	–	9	5	x	4	+	÷	9	4	x	2
=	x	9	4	÷	1	4	9	÷	3	6	÷	9	=	4
3	–	0	9	1	÷	1	5	9	2	2	8	0	–	3
4	÷	9	7	–	–	6	+	=	6	8	1	8	5	2
5	5	7	7	4	0	÷	9	6	2	=	÷	2	2	7
7	÷	÷	x	0	+	7	7	÷	9	8	9	1	8	4
4	8	+	9	5	8	3	5	÷	6	÷	=	4	5	8
2	–	4	1	=	÷	0	0	9	9	3	9	9	2	+
x	5	0	9	2	5	9	7	÷	÷	4	9	÷	8	+
–	3	÷	2	6	8	5	3	8	6	2	7	9	0	+
2	2	+	x	1	0	8	÷	9	=	1	2	=	8	4
7	÷	5	6	2	6	6	7	1	4	+	6	1	÷	1

9÷9=1
18÷9=2
27÷9=3
36÷9=4
45÷9=5
54÷9=6
63÷9=7
72÷9=8
81÷9=9
90÷9=10
99÷9=11
108÷9=12

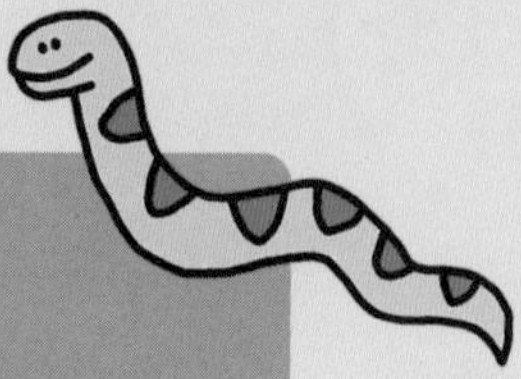

Safari study

The rangers are looking for a herd of equations! Can you help them find the ones in the list?

4	3	3	2	7	÷	9	=	3	1	4	–	1	÷	3
5	8	8	÷	2	÷	8	x	–	3	4	3	9	8	2
÷	+	3	1	2	÷	1	0	7	8	+	4	4	+	1
9	4	4	5	7	5	1	1	5	8	+	7	3	6	4
=	8	x	+	3	x	6	9	4	8	x	2	5	7	5
5	x	6	5	÷	7	1	÷	5	÷	0	2	9	5	x
÷	x	2	8	0	÷	8	=	1	0	1	x	0	1	–
9	÷	3	3	2	÷	8	=	4	=	8	÷	8	=	1
7	9	7	6	÷	÷	÷	=	9	x	5	8	6	4	+
2	x	4	3	0	3	9	÷	8	+	4	7	2	3	9
3	–	3	4	7	÷	8	7	0	0	÷	8	4	x	0
÷	x	0	7	6	0	+	8	9	3	9	5	÷	5	0
5	8	3	3	1	÷	x	2	5	5	=	2	8	2	2
8	4	8	÷	8	=	6	9	6	–	6	8	=	0	+
3	x	1	9	9	÷	9	=	1	1	7	8	3	2	÷

108÷9=12
48÷8=6
99÷9=11
80÷8=10

45÷9=5
8÷8=1
54÷9=6
24÷8=3

36÷9=4
40÷8=5
27÷9=3
32÷8=4

Crash, bang, toot!

The monster music band love equations that divide by eight and nine! Can you find some?

9	0	÷	9	=	1	0	3	2	4	1	6	+	0	x
3	9	÷	+	3	3	5	5	2	5	9	2	5	–	5
2	7	8	9	6	9	1	8	+	4	1	1	5	–	4
0	÷	÷	4	+	7	x	+	6	=	–	5	+	4	–
6	4	÷	8	=	8	4	+	8	1	0	–	0	0	–
6	0	1	9	0	5	4	÷	1	9	2	1	+	3	6
x	5	÷	3	1	3	6	=	+	7	2	÷	8	=	9
2	3	÷	2	4	9	8	x	3	4	–	4	1	+	5
6	3	2	–	+	÷	0	x	3	4	0	7	÷	4	6
8	+	3	2	8	7	8	1	2	2	3	8	9	7	÷
1	3	÷	8	9	8	5	5	=	8	1	3	=	2	8
8	+	÷	0	÷	3	–	8	3	x	3	6	9	÷	=
2	1	x	8	9	1	÷	+	+	7	x	0	x	9	7
2	+	x	8	=	6	0	7	3	9	3	÷	+	=	+
6	7	+	3	1	9	9	1	8	÷	9	=	2	8	8

88÷8=
63÷9=
72÷8=
81÷9=

16÷8=
90÷9=
96÷8=
9÷9=

64÷8=
72÷9=
56÷8=
18÷9=

Traffic jam

What a lot of vehicles! Can you help them to find equations from the eleven times table?

8	4	2	2	4	5	7	8	x	3	5	3	7	1	x
3	x	2	4	2	0	x	1	4	–	9	4	9	2	x
9	1	=	3	–	7	–	0	3	–	1	2	1	3	0
7	1	1	x	1	1	=	1	1	2	–	+	–	1	7
0	=	1	+	5	7	9	3	8	+	7	9	0	=	1
8	4	x	4	4	x	5	8	2	÷	6	7	5	1	0
8	4	2	–	1	x	3	4	8	4	5	7	5	1	x
+	9	3	1	2	0	÷	0	+	=	7	=	=	x	1
+	–	=	6	6	=	1	1	x	6	1	1	1	2	1
÷	9	5	1	1	2	1	=	1	1	x	1	1	1	=
9	x	5	9	9	2	÷	x	4	8	7	x	x	÷	1
3	+	+	1	3	x	1	1	=	3	3	7	5	8	1
0	2	0	4	2	–	3	4	5	–	4	7	2	4	0
7	–	6	6	9	9	2	4	4	8	–	÷	4	–	1
3	7	6	–	3	÷	0	7	+	1	7	0	7	+	+

1x11=11
2x11=22
3x11=33
4x11=44
5x11=55
6x11=66
7x11=77
8x11=88
9x11=99
10x11=110
11x11=121
12x11=132

Farming life

It's a busy day on the farm. We need to find equations from the 12 times table!

–	1	0	1	9	4	–	+	3	9	÷	6	x	8	2
1	4	0	4	3	4	8	=	2	1	x	7	9	8	0
+	1	1	4	3	1	9	7	6	x	÷	6	9	8	6
2	1	+	4	x	1	2	=	4	8	2	–	9	1	=
6	x	4	9	7	+	3	4	+	2	8	6	8	6	2
1	1	–	3	9	+	2	6	÷	3	3	0	x	x	1
x	2	1	2	4	=	1	x	8	=	2	9	1	5	x
1	=	3	4	2	5	6	0	2	1	5	–	2	5	5
2	1	÷	1	÷	x	1	1	=	0	5	3	=	6	x
=	3	x	÷	5	=	x	2	9	7	5	–	9	9	6
1	2	5	0	2	3	1	0	3	2	4	÷	6	3	÷
2	+	9	1	2	x	1	2	=	1	4	4	5	7	5
÷	x	x	7	0	2	7	=	2	1	x	6	9	3	7
9	9	x	1	6	0	7	8	+	2	6	6	+	7	4
2	x	x	2	2	5	9	7	0	5	5	8	0	3	4

1x12=12
2x12=24
3x12=36
4x12=48

5x12=60
6x12=72
7x12=84
8x12=96

9x12=108
10x12=120
11x12=132
12x12=144

11 and 12 times tables

Animal friends

These blue animal friends have come together to solve equations from the 11 and 12 times tables.

8	3	4	6	x	1	1	=	6	6	3	9	–	1	4
2	3	1	=	2	1	x	1	1	9	7	3	3	1	4
+	5	4	9	1	2	9	0	–	x	÷	8	÷	+	1
0	1	1	=	1	1	x	0	1	+	7	5	3	6	=
9	7	7	x	9	+	x	2	–	0	x	2	3	5	2
9	9	3	9	7	÷	=	1	0	1	1	x	9	3	1
÷	x	x	÷	÷	8	7	÷	1	–	–	1	+	–	x
6	5	1	9	4	6	2	=	1	=	x	1	1	9	2
÷	–	0	2	÷	8	5	1	8	9	1	=	2	x	1
7	3	2	2	=	5	=	8	6	x	1	2	=	7	2
8	–	+	8	2	1	+	–	0	5	–	2	1	3	÷
1	7	÷	x	1	5	0	x	3	9	9	1	7	1	9
5	0	8	x	4	8	3	8	3	x	1	2	=	3	6
9	1	1	6	2	7	÷	9	6	6	÷	0	8	3	÷
1	x	1	4	–	8	5	2	3	3	2	5	7	4	4

5x11=55
11x12=132
6x11=66
9x12=108

10x11=110
7x12=84
1x11=11
12x12=144

11x11=121
3x12=36
2x11=22
6x12=72

Art attack!

Open your art box and use your pencils and crayons to mark the equations you find.

4	4	+	2	8	7	9	x	1	1	=	9	9	+	9
÷	9	6	6	2	–	2	x	1	2	=	2	4	–	0
4	8	–	8	–	3	4	x	2	9	+	1	1	6	6
4	9	1	5	x	7	1	4	1	x	0	x	8	1	2
9	4	1	0	x	1	2	=	1	2	0	1	5	3	8
4	6	3	0	8	3	2	÷	1	3	9	2	x	÷	1
2	4	–	6	÷	3	7	=	5	1	÷	=	8	–	4
7	1	1	8	4	=	3	x	9	+	x	1	0	x	4
x	7	1	7	+	1	6	2	1	6	7	2	–	4	=
1	0	÷	3	5	1	+	3	2	2	9	–	1	x	1
1	8	x	8	3	x	+	5	–	5	7	5	4	1	1
=	x	4	–	0	3	5	x	1	2	=	6	0	2	x
7	+	6	8	–	9	8	8	3	3	5	8	0	=	4
7	0	5	0	3	6	9	6	9	x	4	7	7	4	7
1	0	8	2	9	x	4	8	8	=	1	1	x	8	4

10x12=
4x11=
8x12=
8x11=

2x12=
12x11=
1x12=
9x11=

5x12=
7x11=
4x12=
3x11=

Hanging about

It's a jungle out there! We need to find all the equations that divide by eleven before we go home!

÷	3	x	0	3	9	3	3	÷	1	1	=	3	9	8
7	9	0	4	0	6	÷	4	9	2	3	1	3	2	0
7	5	1	7	–	4	6	1	9	1	4	1	x	2	0
÷	1	9	–	÷	6	x	÷	÷	5	1	2	4	÷	4
1	1	9	4	÷	1	÷	9	1	=	3	9	0	1	4
1	0	2	0	7	3	8	8	1	1	3	1	5	1	÷
=	÷	+	–	1	4	7	1	=	÷	=	3	5	=	1
7	1	5	÷	+	9	÷	÷	9	0	1	6	÷	2	1
8	1	6	1	5	1	+	5	2	0	2	–	1	4	=
8	=	0	2	2	1	3	2	÷	1	1	=	1	2	4
1	1	÷	1	1	=	1	2	+	9	5	–	=	x	6
6	0	6	÷	3	÷	7	8	0	1	9	7	5	5	2
8	8	÷	1	1	=	8	4	7	+	5	x	+	9	4
4	÷	–	x	5	+	7	7	x	2	3	–	÷	–	3
1	6	4	+	x	5	5	–	5	7	0	8	1	0	+

11÷11=1
22÷11=2
33÷11=3
44÷11=4

55÷11=5
66÷11=6
77÷11=7
88÷11=8

99÷11=9
110÷11=10
121÷11=11
132÷11=12

Dividing by 12

Laundry time

Learn to divide by twelve with these equations. Can you find them all and sort these socks?

4	x	2	4	÷	6	5	2	8	8	÷	0	6	4	0
4	4	0	6	x	4	1	–	1	2	7	8	4	6	÷
÷	x	x	6	9	9	9	2	2	6	5	1	8	2	2
8	4	÷	1	2	=	7	+	1	0	0	9	÷	3	1
7	6	1	7	7	1	3	2	÷	1	2	=	1	1	2
2	0	–	2	+	3	8	7	–	7	+	2	2	x	0
÷	÷	0	3	÷	5	1	3	9	÷	1	4	=	0	÷
1	1	3	0	–	+	7	4	1	=	5	x	4	–	1
2	2	2	5	+	+	8	3	2	4	÷	1	2	=	2
=	=	–	1	9	=	–	1	2	÷	1	2	=	1	=
6	5	+	+	2	5	÷	6	8	–	1	÷	5	8	1
2	5	3	1	0	4	1	0	8	÷	1	2	=	9	0
2	–	÷	6	4	x	–	7	3	6	÷	1	2	=	3
–	6	8	1	0	4	0	8	2	7	6	1	4	÷	4
9	+	2	9	0	4	6	0	0	–	2	1	7	5	6

12÷12=1
24÷12=2
36÷12=3
48÷12=4
60÷12=5
72÷12=6
84÷12=7
96÷12=8
108÷12=9
120÷12=10
132÷12=11
144÷12=12

Having a kickabout

It's great to play sport! Challenge yourself to find all the equations using eleven and twelve!

2	6	1	5	7	+	6	7	8	4	÷	1	2	=	7
x	÷	5	1	9	÷	=	1	÷	+	÷	+	4	4	0
7	÷	8	5	6	1	7	x	2	÷	7	2	+	2	4
4	8	4	1	1	2	2	2	5	÷	÷	1	x	2	8
+	1	4	÷	2	1	+	0	–	1	1	3	=	6	3
3	0	7	7	6	÷	3	3	x	4	3	2	0	4	7
5	7	+	3	÷	1	5	x	–	x	1	÷	=	9	–
4	8	–	4	9	1	÷	4	8	÷	0	1	4	1	5
6	8	4	8	+	=	6	1	4	2	5	2	8	x	1
9	7	÷	+	9	1	=	2	9	3	7	=	÷	7	9
4	3	3	÷	1	1	=	3	6	6	8	1	1	÷	÷
8	8	÷	1	1	=	8	8	2	3	4	1	2	0	–
5	7	÷	÷	6	–	4	6	0	5	7	7	=	8	3
0	8	1	1	4	4	÷	1	2	=	1	2	4	2	0
0	1	1	1	0	÷	1	1	=	1	0	4	9	1	+

110÷11=10
144÷12=12
121÷11=11
84÷12=7

77÷11=7
132÷12=11
11÷11=1
12÷12=1

88÷11=8
48÷12=4
33÷11=3
24÷12=2

Space explorers

The aliens are visiting! Show them the answers to these division questions, using the grid below.

÷	3	0	9	8	7	3	3	1	8	7	5	6	4	+
+	x	0	+	0	0	−	2	2	+	7	2	9	4	x
5	+	9	8	6	7	−	2	2	0	5	+	6	÷	+
0	4	+	9	7	6	3	1	÷	+	1	6	÷	1	−
5	5	8	9	÷	0	4	6	1	5	4	0	1	1	÷
7	5	6	7	2	1	+	5	1	÷	1	÷	2	=	x
2	2	÷	−	0	5	1	5	=	=	3	1	=	4	1
÷	8	7	1	2	3	−	=	2	1	−	2	8	8	3
1	3	0	5	1	x	5	1	9	0	0	=	+	4	2
2	6	6	−	4	=	÷	2	8	8	9	5	x	1	÷
=	3	8	x	2	0	5	3	6	÷	1	2	=	3	1
6	÷	1	9	2	4	+	4	7	1	7	x	1	0	1
6	6	÷	1	1	=	6	3	4	2	4	8	9	5	=
+	8	4	+	−	x	−	2	+	=	4	÷	−	2	1
6	8	9	1	8	−	5	2	6	9	8	7	7	÷	2

72÷12=
44÷11=
96÷12=
99÷11=

108÷12=
132÷11=
60÷12=
66÷11=

120÷12=
55÷11=
36÷12=
22÷11=

Space adventure

A square number is one number multiplied by itself.
Look at the equations below, then find them in the grid.

7	3	1	9	4	4	8	3	7	x	3	7	8	1	4
7	9	÷	3	7	7	5	7	–	x	2	3	4	2	–
7	x	7	=	4	9	x	5	3	8	2	–	7	1	2
–	0	2	3	3	÷	5	=	0	4	9	8	9	=	1
0	0	5	÷	–	1	9	7	÷	1	0	3	4	1	3
5	2	=	5	x	5	1	3	–	9	9	4	5	1	8
8	8	3	3	1	3	÷	2	1	4	1	–	1	x	6
8	9	x	3	x	7	7	0	6	=	x	0	1	1	3
x	–	1	x	1	8	7	1	2	4	x	4	9	1	5
–	4	8	0	=	0	=	1	x	1	5	6	1	8	+
8	6	=	2	1	4	x	9	0	1	÷	x	1	3	4
2	=	9	4	x	2	5	=	+	–	2	6	5	2	–
5	8	x	4	1	2	1	1	2	6	2	=	4	÷	4
9	x	9	x	8	0	=	5	7	–	7	3	9	7	0
1	8	3	7	0	–	3	4	4	4	7	6	5	5	9

1x1=1
2x2=4
3x3=9
4x4=16
5x5=25
6x6=36
7x7=49
8x8=64
9x9=81
10x10=100
11x11=121
12x12=144

I'm a robot!

The robots work faster with square numbers! Can you find the ones in the list?

x	x	–	9	4	6	7	2	1	–	÷	9	9	x	4
x	1	3	4	4	3	9	2	0	6	9	=	3	x	3
2	1	5	4	0	8	1	6	+	1	5	6	1	2	1
4	÷	3	9	6	=	8	7	4	=	4	÷	7	2	5
2	2	6	2	1	1	5	2	5	4	6	=	8	x	8
5	+	0	1	1	4	÷	5	7	x	3	2	2	–	3
0	–	x	5	4	=	2	x	2	4	=	0	0	8	0
0	1	÷	9	2	÷	1	4	1	x	6	7	3	–	5
1	x	8	x	–	=	9	2	4	0	x	5	9	–	–
=	+	x	9	8	3	5	4	5	÷	6	–	2	6	8
0	÷	2	=	x	x	1	x	9	+	9	5	+	÷	9
1	8	4	8	1	1	8	–	5	9	4	=	7	x	7
x	1	x	1	=	1	x	0	6	7	5	4	8	2	x
0	x	9	6	x	6	6	2	4	8	–	2	1	9	0
1	1	2	x	1	2	=	1	4	4	0	9	2	1	–

1x1=
2x2=
3x3=
4x4=

5x5=
6x6=
7x7=
8x8=

9x9=
10x10=
11x11=
12x12=

Multiplying and dividing 1, 2, 5, 10

At the castle

The knights are battling with a dragon. Can you help them with the equations to defeat the beast?

1	–	x	3	x	x	–	3	+	+	4	–	1	+	+
5	9	8	6	1	3	=	4	4	4	4	9	0	1	6
3	9	–	8	÷	2	+	7	÷	1	=	7	2	6	1
÷	x	+	5	÷	6	8	2	1	2	8	0	5	7	x
8	0	5	6	–	7	x	6	4	÷	–	1	÷	x	1
0	9	0	=	1	7	+	6	8	2	2	2	5	5	2
x	8	5	8	1	5	7	4	7	=	+	x	=	=	x
–	0	5	2	4	5	5	7	1	6	–	2	5	3	5
6	–	3	6	5	8	8	÷	÷	0	+	=	9	5	=
3	2	1	1	=	1	7	–	5	1	–	2	3	–	6
0	÷	1	2	=	9	x	–	0	=	4	4	4	3	0
2	8	÷	2	7	÷	0	2	4	4	1	3	0	6	2
2	6	x	1	0	=	6	0	0	9	5	1	÷	1	3
1	9	x	2	2	8	0	x	–	6	1	x	0	9	8
8	3	2	5	8	÷	0	÷	–	x	9	6	3	÷	1

9x2=18
6÷2=3
12x5=60
25÷5=5

7x5=35
55÷5=11
12x2=24
16÷2=8

6x10=60
7÷1=7
3x5=15
12÷2=6

In a flap

Time for some equation spotting! These use the one, two, five, and ten times tables.

8	x	–	+	8	2	7	3	5	3	0	÷	5	=	6
7	7	1	3	x	+	9	2	2	1	8	6	7	4	÷
5	1	2	0	8	1	=	2	6	2	7	÷	–	6	1
2	÷	2	=	1	5	8	x	1	0	=	8	0	2	1
–	+	5	x	x	9	1	÷	2	÷	0	7	6	1	x
8	2	0	5	4	1	–	9	9	1	3	1	÷	2	1
2	÷	3	1	0	4	0	÷	1	0	=	4	9	1	0
2	1	8	÷	1	7	÷	9	÷	=	4	9	=	x	=
x	x	+	1	1	÷	÷	0	4	1	8	1	4	2	1
2	1	0	÷	5	=	2	0	6	2	x	2	1	6	1
=	4	4	0	5	7	1	x	8	1	7	3	8	÷	0
4	6	4	x	1	x	7	5	1	5	1	3	÷	8	÷
7	6	8	4	2	2	5	1	3	4	–	0	2	8	+
0	0	4	+	7	=	7	5	–	2	9	–	=	0	5
÷	1	2	1	+	x	8	0	4	+	9	2	9	3	÷

10÷5=
11x1=
40÷10=
11x10=

2÷2=
5x5=
120÷10=
4x2=

30÷5=
2x2=
18÷2=
8x10=

Out and about

We're multiplying and dividing using the three and four times tables. Can you find all the equations?

4	+	8	4	4	÷	+	4	–	9	8	2	4	3	3
0	5	3	0	3	–	+	+	÷	÷	1	9	0	+	–
÷	5	6	2	4	÷	4	=	6	6	5	7	3	0	÷
4	9	1	+	2	4	4	6	2	–	7	0	x	4	9
=	5	2	0	x	5	0	5	6	=	0	1	8	–	8
1	0	x	3	=	3	0	6	4	0	–	7	5	÷	5
0	1	4	4	9	6	÷	÷	–	4	0	9	6	2	6
8	0	=	7	=	0	8	x	5	0	2	9	+	9	4
–	7	4	8	4	2	3	4	8	6	1	x	3	=	3
x	4	8	÷	x	÷	0	7	4	+	1	8	6	7	3
x	6	7	1	÷	5	4	1	4	÷	6	5	÷	x	x
6	+	1	x	1	9	3	+	9	7	4	2	3	9	4
5	3	6	1	8	÷	3	=	6	1	6	=	=	÷	=
2	4	x	4	=	1	6	4	0	2	+	4	1	9	1
÷	0	1	–	x	–	4	–	x	5	4	9	2	1	2

10x3=30
18÷3=6
4x4=16
40÷4=10

1x3=3
5x4=20
24÷4=6
44÷4=11

12x4=48
28÷4=7
36÷3=12
3x4=12

Camp out

There's no TV at the campsite, so it's a good thing we've got equations to find!

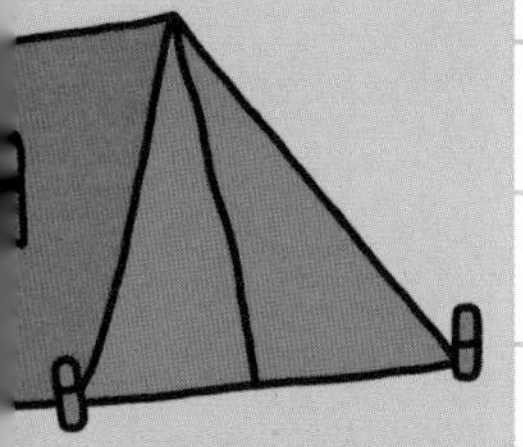

1	5	÷	3	=	5	1	5	3	+	7	x	2	2	+
0	1	0	8	2	÷	3	3	8	x	3	1	1	6	1
2	0	÷	6	1	4	3	=	6	+	÷	1	–	7	1
2	3	+	0	1	7	4	3	x	9	6	x	–	÷	5
–	4	÷	6	4	÷	x	2	3	2	5	4	+	3	7
2	9	÷	1	2	2	8	6	=	6	–	=	8	6	3
2	÷	2	3	+	+	0	–	1	x	9	4	4	2	6
7	x	8	3	=	0	6	2	8	2	0	4	2	3	9
÷	4	1	1	1	8	÷	x	1	5	÷	3	=	1	0
3	6	÷	0	9	–	3	4	7	÷	=	3	+	2	3
=	8	0	7	÷	3	=	=	3	4	x	+	6	÷	9
9	9	–	x	x	–	2	8	x	2	5	7	7	4	0
+	2	–	3	0	÷	2	8	1	2	4	1	4	=	8
x	2	9	+	x	–	5	–	–	4	9	3	0	3	4
9	7	8	9	x	4	=	3	6	÷	3	4	3	8	8

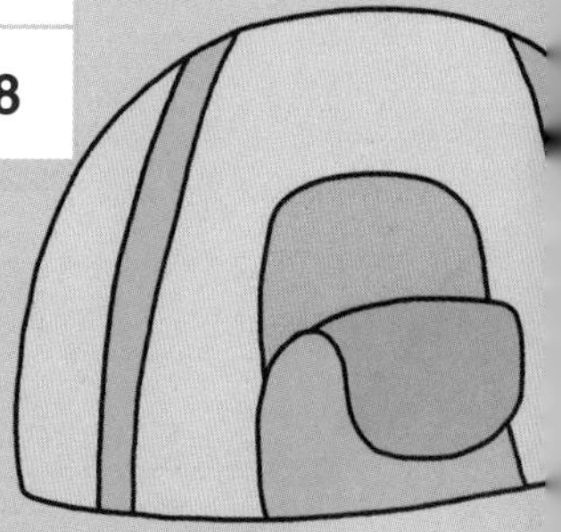

32÷4=
11x4=
15÷3=
2x4=

6÷3=
8x4=
12÷4=
6x3=

24÷3=
12x3=
27÷3=
9x4=

To the rescue!

All the heroes are ready to multiply and divide by six and seven. Let's start!

9	0	1	7	7	x	÷	3	+	8	3	7	÷	1	1
5	3	0	÷	6	=	5	–	8	÷	x	4	–	5	2
1	7	x	x	x	3	x	5	6	2	6	3	0	5	+
7	0	x	4	3	4	8	9	+	2	=	x	x	7	3
5	7	x	7	8	x	7	=	5	6	1	0	x	2	x
+	÷	9	7	=	6	1	9	7	5	8	8	9	÷	5
+	÷	3	2	=	4	3	–	–	5	=	x	6	6	x
4	1	+	3	6	7	9	3	2	7	6	÷	x	=	1
2	2	÷	0	3	8	0	7	÷	=	6	3	6	1	0
7	x	4	4	÷	8	3	6	7	x	2	x	=	2	7
2	7	9	2	7	8	5	÷	x	+	3	2	3	÷	2
6	=	+	9	=	+	2	9	5	x	x	1	6	5	1
0	8	3	8	9	4	8	–	3	0	8	7	–	5	4
0	4	÷	4	x	3	5	1	4	6	÷	+	3	2	+
2	4	–	3	5	0	6	0	÷	6	=	1	0	0	x

56÷7=8
3x6=18
72÷6=12
12x7=84

63÷7=9
10x7=70
42÷7=6
6x6=36

60÷6=10
8x7=56
30÷6=5
7x7=49

In the woods

You have to be quiet when spotting wildlife. Can you keep quiet as you spot these equations, too?

7	x	7	=	4	9	3	÷	9	5	0	3	2	÷	9
7	–	–	x	1	–	5	8	1	+	1	2	5	–	0
8	3	8	x	7	2	2	8	8	2	x	x	x	3	9
6	5	1	÷	7	4	÷	x	0	6	x	0	x	x	0
6	9	0	1	5	5	7	6	5	9	4	6	5	8	÷
÷	7	0	1	3	3	6	5	=	0	x	8	=	8	÷
6	÷	6	1	1	7	+	1	8	2	7	x	3	7	6
=	4	–	2	=	3	8	–	4	+	=	6	–	5	2
1	2	6	6	6	5	+	0	÷	x	2	=	0	5	5
1	+	÷	=	6	4	6	2	7	–	8	4	0	–	9
÷	2	7	4	5	0	5	5	=	2	3	8	7	9	0
4	x	8	=	8	5	4	0	1	–	3	5	+	9	8
9	–	6	6	1	–	9	x	2	2	8	÷	7	=	4
4	x	3	8	1	8	÷	6	=	3	4	+	8	+	0
9	÷	1	9	÷	–	6	1	0	8	1	0	x	9	4

12x6=
12÷6=
7x7=
42÷6=

4x7=
18÷6=
9x6=
28÷7=

9x7=
66÷6=
8x6=
84÷7=

Multiplying and dividing 8 and 9

Octopus birthday

Hiding in this grid are equations using eight and nine. Can you find them all?

6	3	÷	9	=	7	0	÷	8	2	2	9	–	7	7
x	1	0	3	5	4	x	+	6	5	4	5	8	4	5
5	–	8	9	5	2	4	0	4	–	x	1	–	0	–
6	–	x	=	8	6	÷	+	2	÷	4	5	1	÷	5
3	0	9	+	5	+	÷	4	x	7	7	=	2	8	9
7	x	=	6	7	x	6	7	–	0	9	–	x	=	6
6	5	5	8	9	5	8	8	÷	÷	0	7	8	5	2
6	+	2	+	8	+	9	=	0	2	÷	6	=	1	4
–	x	–	0	x	9	0	9	4	2	2	x	9	7	0
2	8	0	x	8	2	9	x	÷	0	x	3	6	3	4
9	9	÷	9	=	1	1	4	8	6	7	÷	8	x	5
4	–	+	6	6	÷	x	5	5	5	–	3	8	8	÷
2	8	0	4	4	3	5	+	1	7	2	÷	8	=	9
3	2	2	8	8	5	5	8	9	8	9	4	8	2	=
6	–	5	5	7	x	8	=	5	6	9	5	6	4	5

40÷8=5
12x8=96
63÷9=7
7x8=56

90÷9=10
8x8=64
72÷8=9
3x8=24

99÷9=11
5x8=40
45÷9=5
6x9=54

All ship shape

Be a true pirate and swashbuckle your way through this list of equations, me hearty!

4	x	9	=	3	6	6	5	1	0	–	5	4	6	–
8	1	2	4	÷	8	=	3	7	9	x	=	1	+	+
7	1	4	1	3	5	5	9	2	1	8	2	+	0	5
5	x	7	x	1	–	3	2	8	÷	9	7	5	5	÷
9	8	0	8	÷	–	2	–	2	÷	9	3	7	x	7
6	=	x	÷	2	8	0	3	9	x	8	=	7	2	6
÷	8	6	8	5	9	9	1	8	–	9	4	x	+	4
8	8	6	6	=	9	–	9	8	–	3	=	x	9	÷
=	2	2	9	–	x	4	8	÷	8	=	6	1	x	8
1	7	x	+	+	2	8	8	8	9	5	8	4	8	=
2	0	4	1	4	1	6	–	x	4	5	x	1	2	8
1	8	÷	9	=	2	9	+	7	+	+	8	–	x	0
5	8	4	5	5	x	÷	5	6	4	x	=	7	–	0
2	+	+	4	7	x	6	x	+	4	3	6	÷	2	8
5	÷	–	4	4	8	+	8	2	9	–	4	–	7	5

8x8=
32÷8=
10x9=
48÷8=

9x8=
96÷8=
11x8=
64÷8=

2x9=
24÷8=
4x9=
18÷9=

Saddle up!

Gee up! It's time to track down some equations that use eleven and twelve.

–	6	1	7	0	8	7	4	6	0	÷	1	2	=	5
1	1	3	7	x	+	0	5	+	+	6	0	3	–	3
5	8	2	5	3	x	x	÷	x	4	1	x	4	8	x
1	x	÷	2	6	2	0	x	6	1	6	1	3	+	2
1	÷	1	+	8	2	6	6	2	0	1	1	9	–	6
x	8	2	4	4	8	÷	7	+	–	1	=	8	9	5
1	+	=	9	7	7	÷	7	3	1	3	1	5	9	6
1	8	1	8	+	3	7	3	1	8	4	1	1	5	6
=	0	1	2	x	=	=	+	9	4	2	0	–	7	2
1	6	8	2	2	1	7	0	8	÷	5	4	5	5	÷
2	2	÷	1	1	=	2	=	4	3	0	9	3	2	4
1	3	÷	x	6	÷	2	=	2	4	÷	1	2	=	2
–	4	3	–	1	1	2	5	9	4	8	8	2	9	÷
8	0	+	6	x	6	3	2	6	6	÷	1	1	=	6
3	+	0	7	3	6	1	9	9	3	0	7	+	6	2

84÷12=7
10x11=110
24÷12=2
11x11=121

66÷11=6
7x12=84
132÷12=11
8x12=96

60÷12=5
5x11=55
22÷11=2
3x11=33

Below the waves

Take a breath and search the grid for the equations that use eleven and twelve, then come up for air!

1	1	÷	÷	+	x	x	1	7	0	6	8	–	÷	–
1	3	9	2	2	2	9	9	4	9	=	6	+	x	6
4	2	0	9	5	+	4	1	3	1	6	0	0	6	–
1	÷	÷	1	x	6	3	7	1	4	1	6	+	0	3
1	1	2	0	1	8	1	÷	1	=	–	7	2	3	1
x	1	9	4	2	5	8	+	1	3	5	7	4	–	0
1	=	5	–	=	8	9	1	4	6	5	9	–	3	8
1	1	÷	+	6	8	÷	9	x	1	1	=	9	9	÷
=	2	6	÷	0	0	0	+	5	4	7	+	–	4	1
1	2	x	3	1	6	2	÷	5	x	3	+	3	4	2
2	0	1	1	9	x	7	x	7	1	9	8	5	÷	=
1	1	x	1	2	=	1	3	2	2	7	8	2	1	9
3	6	÷	1	2	=	3	6	7	=	5	÷	4	1	÷
2	–	x	3	1	+	2	5	5	4	+	6	5	=	7
÷	0	3	4	3	–	3	4	+	8	7	+	2	4	4

11x11=
132÷11=
36÷12=
4x12=

88÷11=
5x12=
11x12=
108÷12=

9x11=
44÷11=
2x12=
110÷11=

Stomp! Chomp! Munch!

Try to find these mixed number equations while the dinosaurs stomp around looking for lunch!

+	1	6	0	7	6	–	2	8	0	0	3	3	4	÷
8	6	+	1	–	5	÷	5	÷	8	+	1	–	4	6
0	6	9	0	6	1	7	1	0	+	0	–	4	2	–
+	7	4	6	1	4	1	7	2	4	x	+	6	1	8
8	1	9	9	=	9	x	1	1	=	5	8	x	2	7
0	÷	8	2	+	9	=	7	8	4	3	–	6	+	1
2	x	+	x	÷	3	9	6	5	4	=	x	8	3	8
5	8	9	8	x	÷	4	0	6	9	=	4	7	–	3
5	5	4	4	3	+	5	2	+	9	4	2	x	–	–
x	–	0	–	x	5	1	5	2	6	5	=	1	1	0
6	÷	0	6	=	7	x	2	x	x	6	2	7	x	9
=	6	5	5	x	8	3	7	0	2	3	=	8	x	4
3	–	x	3	=	9	x	1	0	=	9	0	7	÷	7
0	1	5	4	8	9	+	–	2	1	x	4	5	6	3
1	6	0	8	7	+	÷	+	÷	2	3	9	+	1	1

4x8=32
7x3=21
6x2=12
11x5=55

7x7=49
4x3=12
1x4=4
5x8=40

11x9=99
5x6=30
9x10=90
4x12=48

Caterpillar crawl

These little caterpillars know that equations may be written backward in the grid. Can you find them?

7	8	9	6	–	3	6	8	x	6	2	3	3	8	8
6	5	4	3	6	=	7	x	9	4	x	6	x	1	8
–	÷	–	8	1	0	4	2	1	9	2	6	3	1	2
4	5	7	1	0	1	5	2	=	9	0	2	8	2	8
6	3	2	=	x	9	x	2	2	1	=	4	x	3	9
2	5	2	6	8	6	7	+	3	8	9	0	8	3	2
1	7	÷	x	=	9	7	1	6	4	0	1	–	7	+
1	8	5	3	8	0	2	=	5	x	4	6	1	+	+
7	÷	÷	2	0	0	0	1	4	7	6	1	6	1	9
6	2	0	5	3	1	1	+	9	–	–	4	7	x	=
5	6	x	÷	=	6	x	–	1	4	÷	0	2	x	1
0	4	9	0	+	9	1	+	+	1	0	=	5	9	x
x	8	1	4	6	x	6	=	3	6	1	2	+	6	9
2	x	5	=	1	0	3	–	5	8	–	8	2	7	6
1	1	+	6	7	5	4	6	7	4	2	x	3	=	6

1x10=10
6x6=36
2x5=10
10x8=80

9x1=9
4x5=20
3x6=18
9x7=63

3x9=27
3x4=12
2x3=6
9x2=18

Spot the ghosts!

Hubble bubble, here comes trouble! Find as many equations as you can!

x	5	–	1	x	4	=	4	3	9	0	x	9	÷	–
6	x	1	9	7	÷	6	6	3	4	÷	6	7	÷	9
1	÷	2	9	7	0	=	2	x	9	=	1	8	3	÷
8	6	2	0	–	9	7	2	+	9	1	÷	0	7	x
x	2	+	4	x	4	=	1	6	x	8	2	4	6	7
7	x	2	7	1	÷	4	1	3	9	6	x	5	+	1
=	8	x	9	=	7	2	x	x	7	–	4	x	4	0
5	6	–	3	–	7	8	4	6	x	8	4	7	÷	x
6	6	0	9	9	x	8	=	7	2	1	9	=	÷	4
3	x	4	=	2	4	4	4	=	+	8	4	3	6	=
8	3	1	x	8	÷	÷	4	+	–	4	6	5	6	4
7	x	6	8	6	7	x	1	–	9	3	1	0	+	0
9	2	7	4	1	7	6	÷	4	5	8	9	x	x	x
–	+	x	2	7	5	+	7	+	0	1	+	5	9	6
1	1	x	9	=	9	9	5	3	9	0	1	0	5	1

9x8=
1x4=
11x9=
2x9=

10x4=
9x1=
7x9=
11x4=

8x7=
7x4=
5x7=
4x4=

Safari special

It's great to see animals in the wild. While you are waiting, let's look for some equations!

8	8	4	x	9	=	3	6	2	7	8	0	9	0	5
7	4	6	÷	x	2	8	x	0	1	8	–	0	7	3
1	1	–	÷	1	÷	+	7	9	+	÷	–	8	1	4
2	0	x	6	1	7	6	=	2	1	7	4	x	6	9
–	x	5	–	=	x	÷	4	0	6	7	2	5	3	0
8	2	5	0	9	3	2	2	2	–	5	–	=	÷	9
4	=	÷	–	9	=	8	0	1	9	6	5	4	8	x
6	2	x	1	=	2	6	7	1	6	6	1	0	÷	1
6	0	1	6	x	1	1	x	1	1	=	1	2	1	1
8	5	0	+	3	8	0	9	6	2	1	6	x	+	=
1	9	7	1	÷	6	=	1	x	7	x	2	6	÷	8
3	9	4	÷	4	–	0	8	8	8	3	3	5	9	9
4	x	7	=	2	8	0	4	x	1	0	=	4	0	1
7	x	2	=	1	4	+	6	8	1	3	–	x	x	x
5	–	5	9	8	4	3	8	8	8	+	9	8	4	7

4x7=
10x2=
7x2=
11x11=

1x8=
9x11=
7x3=
8x5=

2x1=
6x7=
4x9=
4x10=

Sound all around

The monster band is playing multiplying music to help you find all the equations below!

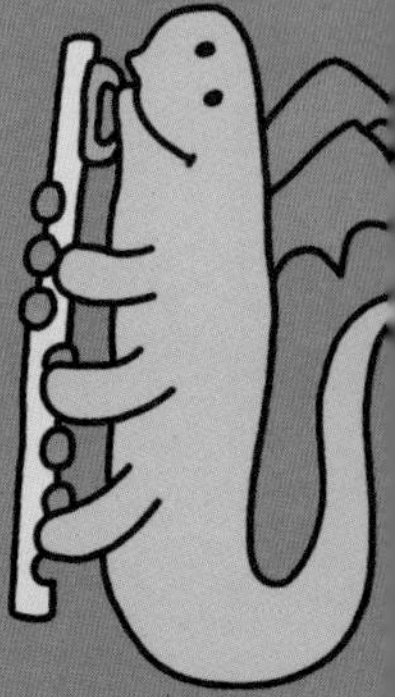

3	3	–	3	÷	–	–	6	4	4	3	+	2	4	6
5	x	7	2	÷	9	0	1	9	–	÷	4	4	7	0
2	3	7	8	x	9	=	7	2	+	6	9	0	5	0
2	4	1	=	2	7	x	5	=	3	5	8	1	x	5
8	+	8	0	2	9	8	x	1	1	2	1	3	6	x
5	9	6	3	1	1	÷	4	4	=	2	0	6	=	1
2	5	3	5	2	1	3	2	7	3	5	x	7	3	1
9	8	5	8	0	3	4	x	8	6	8	5	6	0	=
9	5	4	1	=	1	4	0	3	6	÷	=	x	5	5
0	2	–	1	4	3	3	7	2	–	7	5	9	3	5
2	4	1	x	3	x	÷	x	9	x	1	0	4	÷	6
1	x	+	4	3	1	5	8	9	÷	–	–	7	+	7
3	x	3	5	4	4	2	=	7	9	7	1	9	–	4
4	2	1	=	÷	x	+	5	2	2	0	4	5	0	3
6	÷	–	5	6	3	6	6	=	0	7	8	0	5	4

4x7=
9x7=
8x9=
5x11=

3x7=
4x5=
5x6=
7x8=

2x3=
7x5=
3x11=
10x5=

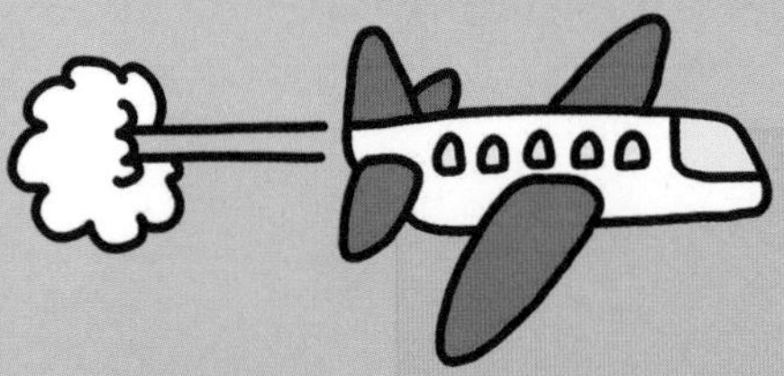

Let's go!

Look at the planes and hot air balloons! Complete the grid and you will be flying high, too!

0	÷	+	4	7	2	÷	6	x	0	5	2	4	0	+
9	8	2	÷	1	4	7	–	8	1	5	9	7	6	0
0	6	0	x	–	6	8	5	8	9	x	+	7	6	9
0	4	+	–	0	3	÷	2	5	3	1	8	x	9	–
–	0	3	8	÷	x	9	1	2	7	9	0	6	5	8
0	x	+	x	6	6	6	2	1	–	5	0	=	0	+
0	5	7	+	1	=	7	9	3	4	x	9	4	x	8
9	3	8	2	x	1	+	÷	8	6	3	x	2	9	x
x	0	4	–	4	8	=	2	÷	9	=	3	8	x	6
6	3	1	6	2	x	4	3	6	x	1	=	6	8	÷
=	6	0	7	3	x	1	=	3	÷	5	2	1	=	3
5	+	3	2	9	8	÷	–	x	4	x	7	5	7	0
4	8	x	+	+	–	8	7	x	4	=	2	8	2	1
–	9	–	3	+	0	–	3	8	1	4	x	2	=	8
1	0	x	2	=	2	0	2	x	5	÷	9	4	0	1

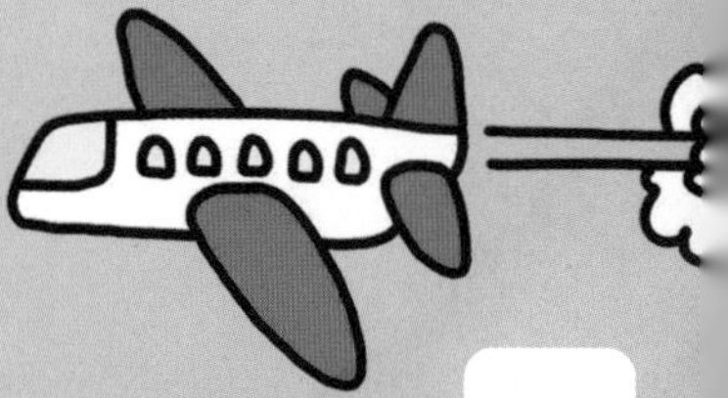

6x1=
7x6=
3x1=
9x6=

5x3=
3x6=
10x2=
3x11=

9x8=
9x3=
4x2=
7x4=

Friendly farm

All of the equations below use division. Can you find them in the grid?

9	0	7	9	4	3	3	+	+	÷	3	2	0	5	2
+	÷	9	=	1	+	–	6	9	3	4	5	0	9	6
4	2	x	1	2	4	x	x	–	8	x	6	0	3	=
+	–	x	÷	9	7	2	3	0	1	=	4	÷	0	4
2	1	5	9	4	2	6	8	÷	3	+	–	4	3	÷
8	x	0	8	5	÷	5	5	0	5	6	+	x	x	4
9	8	7	÷	6	8	–	–	7	2	x	+	+	0	2
5	–	5	=	1	5	8	6	8	+	6	9	2	9	8
7	=	6	0	4	=	6	9	8	7	3	1	0	0	7
5	2	9	9	8	÷	1	3	÷	3	÷	7	÷	7	x
0	=	3	9	6	–	8	0	8	+	x	÷	5	1	9
5	5	1	÷	8	–	–	2	=	2	+	0	=	5	x
5	÷	3	7	9	7	x	–	1	5	4	9	4	+	4
4	0	x	5	8	x	0	÷	1	=	1	÷	1	1	5
9	1	x	x	1	0	0	÷	1	0	=	1	0	+	5

28÷4=7
10÷5=2
9÷1=9
24÷4=6

1÷1=1
88÷8=11
100÷10=10
40÷4=10

20÷5=4
36÷6=6
10÷1=10
25÷5=5

Mixed dividing

Gorgeous green

There are lots of equations to find in this grid.
Read the list, then search!

9	8	–	÷	0	1	9	1	0	4	8	÷	6	=	8
7	3	6	3	÷	7	=	9	5	5	÷	5	–	÷	0
8	3	6	÷	6	=	6	÷	6	2	5	3	+	1	3
4	1	4	9	9	8	5	3	6	6	1	4	0	5	–
9	=	1	÷	9	=	4	2	÷	1	=	–	4	5	–
8	2	1	÷	9	6	6	8	9	=	1	+	x	÷	=
÷	8	÷	3	x	4	=	3	7	6	1	9	2	9	x
÷	8	8	3	6	7	5	x	5	3	÷	7	=	8	1
÷	5	1	÷	0	3	÷	6	4	4	1	0	2	=	6
9	4	4	3	1	2	÷	3	=	4	1	x	4	9	+
4	+	–	=	+	6	5	+	1	÷	8	1	8	÷	+
x	3	=	1	1	÷	=	3	0	3	2	1	9	2	7
0	7	8	1	+	2	0	9	+	+	8	+	4	7	x
÷	0	0	5	2	0	7	4	÷	6	5	x	6	9	4
8	–	0	1	=	7	÷	0	7	x	8	3	÷	7	4

56÷8=7
48÷6=8
33÷3=11
72÷9=8

36÷6=6
11÷11=1
90÷10=9
63÷7=9

9÷1=9
70÷7=10
45÷5=9
12÷3=4

Get creative!

Let's add some fun to this grid with yellow, purple, and pink. Find the equations and circle them!

9	3	4	÷	7	5	+	9	9	4	7	6	2	1	8
5	3	x	6	2	=	4	2	5	+	=	8	6	7	–
4	3	9	6	÷	5	0	9	+	6	9	1	0	7	÷
5	÷	9	9	8	÷	7	1	4	3	5	0	÷	4	x
0	3	+	–	=	5	7	0	=	6	÷	3	2	4	0
9	=	3	÷	9	2	–	7	7	0	1	7	+	0	7
2	1	4	8	÷	x	+	–	4	1	1	3	9	=	2
9	1	+	÷	2	5	5	7	=	7	4	÷	5	4	x
6	7	–	+	7	5	8	1	0	7	7	÷	0	7	1
2	1	÷	7	=	3	1	+	3	5	5	+	0	0	9
÷	0	÷	9	8	÷	÷	0	2	3	=	1	8	0	1
8	7	–	9	1	7	4	÷	÷	8	4	9	6	4	3
0	x	1	2	7	4	–	–	4	2	÷	÷	÷	–	3
8	+	1	2	0	+	4	9	=	5	0	3	2	5	÷
4	2	0	2	9	1	0	÷	8	8	2	÷	2	9	4

33÷3=
72÷8=
4÷1=
121÷11=

100÷10=
21÷7=
35÷5=
45÷9=

9÷3=
25÷5=
20÷4=
32÷4=

Tropical wildlife

These jungle animals are having fun dividing numbers. They need your help to find the equations.

1	+	÷	1	6	x	7	5	0	x	4	9	–	x	2
8	4	1	1	6	3	3	1	+	6	9	4	9	6	–
9	+	1	+	6	÷	+	6	0	–	9	8	2	7	8
2	+	=	÷	7	8	9	÷	3	÷	3	3	4	+	6
1	+	3	1	–	9	9	÷	1	7	1	+	÷	7	+
÷	3	÷	3	x	÷	2	6	1	7	9	0	3	÷	2
7	÷	3	6	÷	2	=	3	=	9	4	4	=	1	5
=	x	3	4	9	2	8	9	–	2	=	6	8	1	4
3	x	2	8	=	5	÷	9	0	1	÷	2	1	3	=
–	7	9	9	9	3	6	0	1	4	2	7	x	÷	8
5	2	÷	7	6	–	1	÷	5	2	8	4	+	9	÷
0	8	5	9	+	–	4	4	6	0	9	÷	3	+	2
1	8	7	5	0	4	6	4	÷	8	=	8	3	0	3
÷	0	9	0	÷	x	5	9	7	6	8	5	6	+	÷
÷	1	+	7	1	3	–	3	5	=	7	÷	5	3	+

21÷7=
18÷9=
35÷7=
10÷10=

64÷8=
44÷11=
32÷8=
6÷2=

33÷3=
16÷8=
24÷3=
63÷9=

On your feet!

These equations will keep you on your toes! Let's get to work!

1	+	3	8	x	3	5	2	9	2	3	1	0	÷	3
5	3	=	2	÷	6	x	1	0	1	=	6	÷	0	6
2	–	4	6	6	9	9	1	7	0	x	6	6	+	1
7	1	2	4	x	+	+	=	4	1	8	1	4	4	8
9	8	2	7	1	÷	8	8	1	2	=	–	4	3	6
2	3	9	÷	+	4	1	÷	=	7	2	4	2	–	2
x	6	+	6	2	2	÷	8	7	x	1	4	0	9	8
2	x	8	+	7	=	÷	8	4	÷	÷	2	5	8	1
6	4	x	2	+	6	6	1	9	5	6	–	2	–	6
6	0	9	1	1	=	4	÷	4	4	9	7	8	4	2
x	=	2	÷	2	1	–	x	0	8	6	1	5	0	5
–	5	6	+	3	3	7	–	0	3	6	÷	÷	4	2
6	4	0	÷	4	=	1	0	2	3	9	5	9	6	÷
8	0	÷	9	6	3	7	1	+	=	=	–	÷	2	6
7	=	5	÷	5	3	6	7	5	4	x	+	7	3	+

6÷2=
44÷4=
36÷6=
45÷9=

12÷2=
88÷8=
96÷12=
60÷6=

40÷4=
20÷5=
35÷5=
16÷8=

Score that goal!

Let's have a kickabout with numbers! Find the dividing equations in the grid.

4	2	÷	6	=	7	2	–	7	÷	7	5	7	2	4
2	–	+	1	0	8	1	0	7	5	+	–	8	6	3
0	÷	0	–	8	7	8	6	7	2	–	+	6	9	1
1	1	=	2	÷	2	2	5	4	7	÷	+	=	4	x
4	–	7	1	7	6	6	2	0	x	÷	9	1	7	4
3	÷	4	6	2	÷	÷	+	2	1	÷	7	=	3	4
x	1	9	1	5	0	5	0	5	1	=	6	÷	8	÷
–	6	–	7	1	5	2	=	8	4	x	5	8	+	+
÷	7	5	x	=	2	=	=	1	7	1	9	÷	+	7
2	–	÷	5	0	0	÷	8	2	1	0	5	7	0	9
8	÷	x	1	1	5	1	3	÷	÷	÷	7	2	÷	5
7	1	0	6	7	6	4	÷	=	0	4	5	0	9	9
9	6	7	x	7	2	–	3	0	4	4	7	5	5	3
–	8	=	4	÷	2	3	÷	2	7	÷	7	2	9	6
8	+	6	6	2	3	+	1	2	÷	6	=	2	9	9

70÷10=
40÷8=
4÷2=
12÷3=

81÷9=
42÷6=
12÷6=
72÷9=

22÷2=
50÷5=
55÷11=
32÷4=

Life on Mars!

Here's a list of mixed dividing and multiplying equations for a real astronaut ace!

3	3	3	÷	8	–	4	4	0	=	6	8	0	0	2
x	=	6	3	÷	4	=	0	7	x	9	6	7	5	5
8	÷	4	2	4	0	2	0	6	2	2	3	1	2	1
9	4	4	÷	3	8	÷	2	6	=	+	+	1	5	1
+	5	3	=	2	7	8	5	0	3	+	=	8	0	1
3	6	5	–	=	1	1	8	0	9	6	1	3	4	2
÷	x	1	1	x	5	=	5	5	÷	7	5	–	÷	=
6	7	0	0	8	8	3	–	2	8	9	4	÷	÷	7
0	8	x	x	4	÷	7	7	=	5	6	0	x	8	x
9	6	4	3	–	4	6	9	3	x	9	5	6	3	3
5	1	2	=	x	x	÷	=	9	2	0	3	5	1	3
7	9	3	3	0	2	0	=	3	÷	9	7	4	7	5
+	8	4	0	7	x	5	+	÷	1	6	9	4	÷	0
5	5	3	x	4	4	x	6	7	4	4	x	1	=	4
2	0	8	–	2	6	x	0	9	9	1	0	1	4	0

18÷6=
6x5=
72÷6=
3x7=

8÷2=
6x9=
12÷4=
11x5=

72÷9=
10x3=
70÷7=
4x1=

Explore the galaxy

3 ... 2 ... 1 ... blast off! Time to find these mixed equations in the list below!

7	÷	6	1	8	1	+	1	1	1	x	6	=	6	4
8	=	3	9	1	2	1	7	÷	6	7	x	9	4	9
0	9	7	+	7	7	–	1	1	÷	÷	+	x	9	÷
÷	6	8	=	1	÷	x	8	0	x	0	4	4	1	7
÷	–	9	8	1	7	÷	8	÷	÷	–	0	=	+	=
9	x	6	5	–	6	1	7	=	7	1	÷	3	4	7
8	=	3	–	=	–	x	5	÷	5	+	=	7	6	2
1	8	÷	3	7	5	5	–	6	0	6	4	1	3	3
1	7	1	1	x	5	=	5	5	7	+	2	3	0	=
=	0	=	–	4	8	4	2	÷	9	7	5	+	9	÷
3	÷	2	4	=	9	1	3	8	5	8	x	÷	–	1
÷	5	x	7	÷	2	3	=	4	x	8	3	3	x	+
3	7	÷	+	÷	8	7	2	4	–	–	7	1	0	0
3	6	5	7	÷	7	2	7	4	2	=	4	x	6	0
5	8	8	1	4	4	0	0	6	6	6	÷	0	3	0

10÷1=
49÷7=
28÷4=
8x4=

56÷7=
6x4=
18÷6=
11x5=

33÷3=
1x6=
16÷4=
8x9=

Tech trouble

These times tables bots are busy with calculations! Can you help them find the equations in the grid?

4	1	4	4	÷	1	2	=	1	2	4	x	6	6	–
8	1	3	7	4	4	9	–	3	7	4	3	0	8	2
x	1	+	3	4	2	6	=	0	1	÷	0	6	=	3
5	÷	4	5	–	3	=	5	÷	5	1	8	4	2	–
+	8	7	2	8	÷	7	4	3	9	4	0	0	÷	1
2	1	7	4	8	4	6	–	=	5	4	+	1	6	x
–	1	5	3	2	9	x	x	1	6	x	5	=	1	+
7	9	=	=	=	8	7	÷	0	–	8	1	7	5	=
÷	0	6	2	+	7	–	–	4	x	3	=	÷	4	4
7	x	+	2	x	+	÷	0	1	–	x	3	0	+	–
4	5	=	9	x	6	8	1	–	7	1	x	7	1	1
+	+	+	6	2	9	=	8	2	6	1	=	÷	+	–
4	9	5	7	8	8	2	9	1	3	=	x	1	–	÷
8	2	2	÷	8	5	8	1	7	1	3	3	3	6	2
9	–	0	1	=	x	3	0	7	+	3	÷	+	+	2

60÷10=
4x6=
15÷5=
6x2=

21÷7=
8x11=
30÷3=
6x9=

70÷7=
144÷12=
16÷2=
3x11=

Knight time

Challenge the dragon to a duel of numbers with this equation search!

8	2	x	9	4	4	2	7	1	8	÷	8	=	1	1
0	4	3	9	4	4	4	4	8	5	–	4	2	9	–
÷	x	x	1	6	=	1	÷	0	7	9	3	7	4	2
1	–	9	÷	1	÷	7	4	6	–	6	4	x	4	0
0	1	=	2	9	0	+	x	3	x	6	1	5	6	5
=	2	2	8	9	=	x	x	7	4	÷	=	3	3	7
8	1	7	4	1	÷	4	1	+	4	6	7	6	+	0
5	=	–	3	5	4	4	÷	1	0	=	x	8	2	4
x	4	7	0	3	5	6	–	6	=	1	2	+	7	6
7	x	6	3	+	÷	2	2	8	3	1	+	2	x	6
÷	3	8	÷	3	9	–	7	0	–	6	1	2	1	2
÷	0	8	÷	÷	=	4	5	÷	1	8	5	0	1	5
7	x	x	4	4	5	4	3	7	+	1	2	9	=	5
5	1	2	x	5	=	+	3	x	8	9	0	x	7	8
÷	1	8	5	+	÷	2	÷	÷	4	0	8	6	7	5

8÷8=
7x7=
8÷4=
3x4=

66÷6=
2x7=
45÷9=
10x11=

36÷4=
3x9=
80÷10=
7x11=

Winging it!

Stretch your wings with this puzzle! Find the equations listed below in the grid.

–	1	6	9	7	3	7	3	x	7	1	÷	9	2	3
8	=	1	x	8	0	1	5	1	7	8	1	+	8	9
5	4	7	8	–	1	9	x	5	4	1	0	1	9	8
5	4	2	2	x	9	=	1	8	2	÷	÷	2	+	x
+	+	3	=	=	x	1	=	–	8	9	2	8	0	5
6	5	1	–	4	4	4	5	÷	3	=	2	=	5	4
5	3	2	3	3	x	÷	2	x	1	9	÷	1	7	÷
8	2	3	÷	0	2	6	7	x	3	3	8	x	4	6
8	1	6	÷	8	=	2	2	=	x	0	2	5	5	=
5	5	÷	1	1	=	5	x	+	2	÷	5	0	2	9
+	÷	÷	2	5	÷	x	3	3	0	8	7	7	=	2
–	8	5	x	÷	7	5	–	+	7	9	5	6	5	0
2	7	x	7	4	1	1	6	0	0	2	1	2	x	=
4	7	5	7	8	4	x	1	1	=	4	4	2	5	5
9	3	6	=	3	÷	8	1	=	5	÷	5	=	1	1

14÷2=
2x9=
81÷9=
8x1=

18÷3=
4x11=
16÷8=
5x5=

55÷11=
6x4=
54÷6=
5x1=

Dive in!

Sploosh! After a dive in the ocean, it's time to find equations. Let's hope there aren't any sharks!

–	9	9	8	5	9	x	1	2	=	1	0	8	6	4
8	5	1	9	÷	7	3	=	7	÷	–	3	5	=	6
0	5	6	7	7	7	3	x	x	6	2	2	–	5	1
1	1	x	1	=	1	1	3	1	3	7	8	5	=	1
4	9	8	+	1	0	+	=	2	9	6	÷	3	3	x
7	2	8	1	–	3	x	2	÷	÷	÷	+	8	0	1
9	5	7	x	6	4	3	7	2	3	1	–	0	2	1
6	5	+	–	2	7	÷	9	=	3	5	2	7	1	=
1	+	÷	–	7	=	8	+	6	–	+	=	=	4	1
x	5	8	3	0	5	1	6	÷	1	5	2	÷	x	2
7	2	3	2	0	÷	4	6	x	÷	÷	6	÷	1	1
=	9	7	9	4	÷	8	2	5	2	6	2	4	0	x
7	7	2	4	5	2	5	3	2	3	5	7	–	2	+
0	x	2	3	8	2	–	=	2	4	2	4	5	8	÷
5	4	÷	6	=	9	+	+	6	3	x	4	=	1	2

30÷5=
11x11=
54÷6=
11x1=

12÷2=
8x2=
35÷5=
3x4=

22÷2=
9x12=
27÷9=
1x7=

Set up camp

If you're ready for a night camping under the stars, you're ready for this puzzle, too!

2	2	1	3	2	÷	1	1	=	1	2	=	9	x	9
8	1	=	8	5	6	–	6	3	–	3	3	7	4	1
0	7	8	8	2	3	6	0	1	6	5	1	1	+	x
2	+	÷	3	0	–	4	–	1	1	7	2	2	x	6
8	7	8	x	÷	7	7	1	7	8	3	1	1	6	÷
=	5	8	4	8	6	=	6	6	5	x	–	0	8	0
7	3	1	8	9	2	5	7	2	9	2	5	9	x	2
÷	=	+	6	÷	6	3	6	÷	1	=	÷	=	0	=
7	7	+	2	7	÷	x	6	÷	9	6	3	0	9	2
=	x	2	–	=	1	5	x	9	=	4	5	1	0	x
1	5	2	6	2	+	2	7	÷	6	3	5	x	7	0
1	5	x	÷	÷	8	4	÷	÷	1	1	6	9	0	1
=	÷	1	5	4	7	7	÷	1	1	=	7	4	3	÷
8	3	x	1	1	=	3	3	x	÷	x	0	8	0	8
+	÷	1	1	9	0	3	–	6	3	0	6	6	+	–

49÷7=
3x2=
8÷8=
3x11=

14÷2=
10x2=
132÷11=
5x7=

77÷7=
5x9=
22÷2=
9x10=

Mixed equations

Save the day!

The superheroes are here to help! They've made a list of equations for you to find in the grid!

0	2	1	9	3	2	x	5	1	6	–	4	÷	7	–
5	0	–	4	+	6	3	5	÷	6	+	4	÷	+	4
3	÷	÷	5	–	9	1	–	7	9	x	÷	9	7	4
=	2	8	4	x	1	9	6	÷	4	0	1	7	6	÷
5	=	x	=	x	4	3	÷	9	1	0	1	3	÷	1
x	1	6	5	+	2	4	=	=	8	8	=	2	0	1
7	0	=	x	1	4	5	0	1	1	5	4	–	–	5
÷	5	4	9	0	8	1	8	x	1	+	x	x	1	–
5	6	8	=	8	÷	4	6	–	9	÷	7	2	1	÷
1	–	7	3	0	8	=	2	–	=	5	3	8	7	0
5	–	2	0	1	÷	÷	5	x	9	x	+	3	4	–
3	9	1	7	7	–	9	5	8	x	0	0	=	9	3
4	1	9	+	4	x	=	6	+	1	6	5	5	3	÷
–	7	–	x	x	÷	5	5	6	+	x	2	7	6	1
7	2	÷	9	=	8	=	1	8	8	5	1	4	1	3

72÷9=
8x6=
33÷11=
9x5=

64÷8=
1x9=
100÷10=
8x5=

20÷2=
7x5=
44÷11=
11x5=

Spotting squirrels

Squirrels aren't the only things hiding here. Can you find the list of equations, too?

÷	3	1	6	9	÷	÷	7	9	+	7	4	4	2	5
8	7	2	7	x	6	7	x	2	=	1	4	+	5	–
=	÷	0	9	8	4	8	9	0	8	x	+	7	x	2
1	9	+	+	3	9	=	1	4	0	6	–	0	7	1
3	–	7	–	8	9	0	2	+	2	8	5	÷	=	9
2	9	3	x	9	5	3	3	4	3	4	0	7	3	2
÷	1	x	9	÷	3	x	7	2	9	2	9	=	5	9
1	6	4	6	=	7	1	3	2	2	÷	3	1	9	–
2	÷	3	6	3	+	=	8	4	3	6	x	0	+	x
=	+	÷	7	0	4	3	+	÷	6	=	8	5	x	5
1	8	÷	5	x	6	8	5	8	2	7	+	0	6	÷
1	2	x	8	7	8	–	7	=	4	=	x	2	7	7
1	+	0	8	3	8	=	4	3	x	–	9	3	÷	÷
÷	7	0	5	0	x	÷	5	7	6	2	2	3	7	÷
1	1	x	2	=	2	2	6	6	÷	0	+	+	0	8

132÷12=
6x4=
24÷8=
8x4=

18÷6=
11x2=
70÷7=
5x7=

42÷6=
7x8=
18÷2=
7x2=

Octopus disco

Turn on the music and we're ready to dance!
Let's get started finding equations.

1	5	5	5	0	x	−	+	4	9	9	7	7	9	6
1	9	4	2	6	4	3	0	5	2	9	2	2	5	6
7	÷	1	4	2	÷	8	6	6	x	x	5	−	4	−
1	8	5	9	9	=	8	÷	2	8	8	6	=	4	x
1	2	x	4	8	5	3	=	8	÷	+	5	=	1	÷
x	2	x	x	9	5	0	7	7	=	÷	0	0	1	7
1	3	0	0	6	x	÷	3	8	0	6	9	8	8	2
1	1	1	+	+	7	3	2	2	3	x	+	−	7	6
=	7	7	9	x	9	=	8	1	6	4	8	x	÷	9
1	4	2	0	1	5	1	6	+	÷	=	2	÷	9	0
2	4	6	8	4	−	0	3	5	÷	2	3	7	8	2
1	1	1	−	3	3	9	9	−	6	4	6	5	x	x
8	1	÷	0	0	3	3	8	x	7	1	5	3	6	1
4	4	÷	4	=	1	1	4	2	÷	6	=	7	4	=
1	0	2	2	x	1	9	8	2	9	7	9	8	1	2

20÷5=
2x6=
56÷8=
11x11=

44÷4=
10x8=
42÷6=
9x9=

30÷3=
2x1=
48÷8=
6x4=

Captain's orders

Captain Badnumber has ordered us to find the equations! Better get started or we'll have to walk the plank!

2	–	0	2	2	÷	2	=	1	1	0	÷	x	1	5
x	8	4	3	5	6	6	6	5	x	7	=	3	5	9
5	9	4	÷	x	÷	=	x	5	1	–	+	+	6	+
=	1	5	2	4	9	3	8	0	3	7	3	6	1	1
1	8	–	4	÷	÷	–	4	÷	x	5	2	4	5	5
0	9	1	4	2	7	7	–	5	1	6	x	5	2	÷
3	–	5	2	÷	8	=	÷	=	1	÷	9	1	4	÷
x	+	x	x	5	1	5	6	1	=	8	=	4	4	8
4	3	6	7	9	x	–	8	0	3	=	1	x	=	9
3	+	2	=	7	÷	3	6	1	3	7	8	4	2	4
7	3	5	1	4	6	=	0	7	2	x	x	÷	–	8
x	÷	8	4	7	5	3	8	8	4	2	7	2	9	x
1	8	3	8	÷	6	–	x	6	0	3	x	6	÷	3
–	5	0	0	9	1	x	6	x	÷	4	÷	2	4	4
6	–	3	7	3	2	9	÷	÷	7	5	3	0	3	3

54÷9=
2x7=
22÷2=
5x7=

50÷5=
3x11=
56÷8=
2x4=

30÷5=
2x5=
42÷7=
2x9=

Riding west

You can ride off into the sunset when you've finished finding these mixed equations. Yee ha!

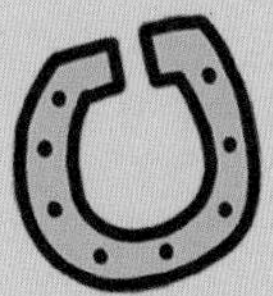

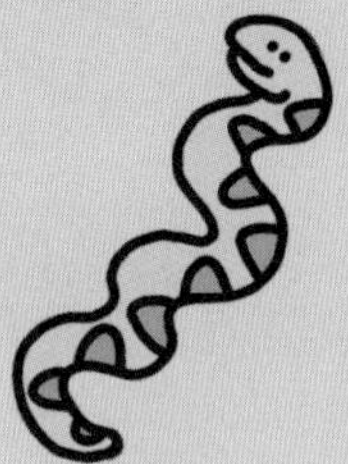

3	6	0	3	6	+	3	5	5	+	5	5	x	7	0
7	2	4	8	7	0	4	=	4	1	0	0	8	0	4
9	÷	0	7	÷	8	1	3	7	x	5	4	–	4	+
8	4	8	3	÷	x	4	x	x	+	3	÷	=	+	0
7	2	9	9	5	0	–	4	3	÷	+	4	2	5	4
0	2	9	÷	÷	–	0	=	=	0	x	–	1	x	9
1	5	÷	0	7	0	8	1	2	1	x	÷	8	3	8
1	+	x	9	3	=	+	2	1	5	2	x	÷	=	9
0	9	1	+	=	1	7	9	9	4	8	2	3	1	–
÷	÷	6	8	9	8	÷	5	5	9	8	8	=	5	3
1	1	8	0	2	5	÷	5	=	5	9	÷	6	0	0
0	+	3	2	x	1	0	=	2	0	7	2	6	3	÷
=	+	4	x	÷	5	1	5	0	–	÷	0	9	–	5
1	1	0	8	5	1	4	7	8	–	7	0	x	0	=
1	6	2	4	2	6	0	1	7	5	8	0	8	2	6

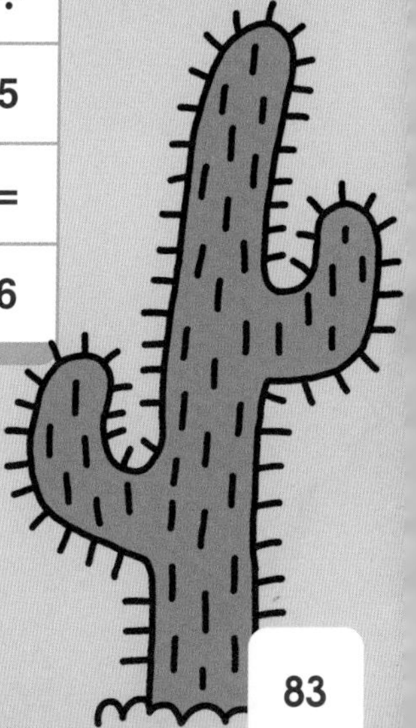

49÷7=
3x4=
18÷3=
11x4=

110÷10=
5x3=
30÷5=
7x3=

72÷9=
5x1=
25÷5=
2x10=

Mixed equations

A sunny day

The sky is blue, the birds are singing! See how many of these equations you can find in the grid.

9	2	+	2	9	7	4	4	4	8	7	=	7	2	0
÷	4	5	+	x	2	8	7	x	7	3	+	x	2	2
1	÷	7	÷	+	x	x	7	x	÷	0	1	7	5	3
–	3	5	4	+	3	3	x	2	1	3	0	=	1	=
5	=	8	9	1	3	x	4	1	–	1	2	4	÷	7
x	8	5	=	4	9	5	1	2	6	9	=	9	6	÷
+	x	5	1	÷	4	=	3	3	=	9	÷	7	2	1
6	5	3	1	7	9	1	8	0	x	–	÷	2	7	2
7	x	1	÷	=	1	5	3	1	6	0	5	÷	x	9
8	x	3	9	2	2	+	3	2	8	–	0	5	0	4
6	7	4	9	–	9	9	4	9	5	=	–	÷	x	2
–	+	–	8	3	x	+	+	8	5	÷	9	7	4	4
8	4	2	1	8	÷	÷	–	7	7	=	=	x	5	4
9	1	7	4	4	6	+	3	3	1	2	+	+	9	5
8	5	1	0	x	3	=	3	0	8	3	7	–	6	2

24÷3=
3x5=
27÷9=
10x3=

99÷11=
4x7=
90÷9=
7x7=

21÷7=
9x9=
14÷7=
7x11=

A land long ago

Multiply and divide with the dinosaur gang. They'll cheer you on as you find these equations!

x	5	1	+	5	9	7	1	6	6	0	9	0	8	+
0	1	8	0	9	x	9	x	1	3	–	x	2	x	5
7	2	÷	5	8	5	5	9	–	x	4	x	6	9	8
x	7	3	5	1	3	6	2	÷	2	4	2	5	=	0
5	÷	=	÷	1	6	7	4	0	x	0	=	9	7	÷
6	9	6	5	+	6	6	3	÷	4	1	2	4	2	2
+	=	+	=	–	0	2	÷	7	8	–	6	9	4	–
4	3	3	1	1	x	x	+	1	7	=	9	÷	3	–
8	5	2	1	2	5	8	1	5	6	–	8	7	8	4
7	7	1	3	3	1	8	7	5	6	4	4	=	÷	3
7	4	0	=	÷	0	8	÷	÷	5	÷	6	7	6	8
2	5	7	1	5	4	5	6	=	3	8	7	3	7	8
6	x	9	=	5	4	6	6	–	–	8	8	=	7	5
5	6	5	0	÷	–	x	3	3	÷	+	÷	+	8	–
7	x	=	=	4	9	=	4	x	4	=	1	6	0	3

27÷9=
11x4=
64÷8=
5x7=

49÷7=
4x4=
55÷5=
8x9=

18÷3=
9x6=
56÷7=
6x9=

Bug party

They may be tiny, but these creepy crawlies are big fans of multiplication and division. Just like you!

−	=	8	+	3	3	4	2	8	6	2	x	7	7	4
x	9	8	x	0	2	6	2	3	5	÷	5	=	7	2
2	8	5	1	3	−	0	4	8	7	5	0	x	x	2
2	4	7	0	=	2	7	0	4	6	9	6	8	6	9
÷	3	8	3	8	3	÷	x	1	3	7	=	÷	9	4
7	0	÷	=	2	÷	x	4	x	=	1	6	1	5	9
1	−	9	6	=	x	2	6	=	6	0	2	8	=	9
1	1	9	x	6	4	9	÷	9	8	5	1	1	0	−
6	4	0	5	÷	+	6	=	7	−	=	÷	x	+	+
4	9	7	6	2	3	5	3	1	2	9	2	6	0	x
0	÷	4	7	1	0	0	5	7	8	=	−	÷	6	1
x	7	0	−	6	÷	0	3	3	3	0	9	3	x	÷
9	=	0	+	6	2	9	1	5	−	0	÷	x	1	−
8	7	7	=	0	7	÷	6	9	6	+	3	+	3	1
1	7	5	4	8	0	4	5	+	2	0	5	−	7	÷

6x3=
32÷4=
2x9=
12÷6=

5x6=
9÷1=
10x10=
49÷7=

3x9=
35÷5=
2x8=
30÷6=

SOLUTIONS

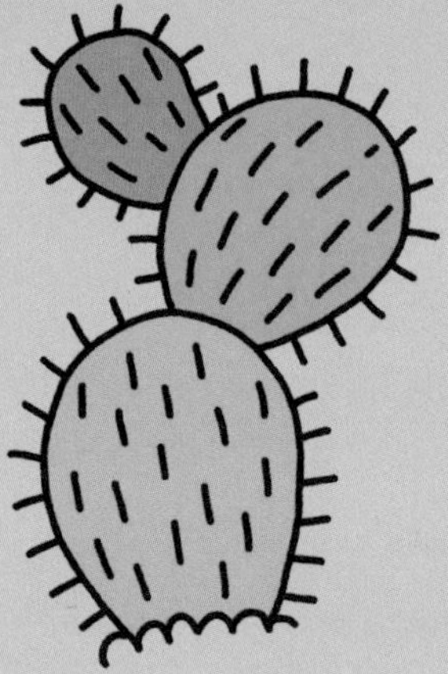

PAGE 4

÷	4	9	1	2	x	1	=	1	2	÷	2	5	5	1
−	9	2	5	−	+	+	6	4	x	2	−	7	9	÷
+	6	0	=	6	7	2	0	x	9	1	7	6	2	3
x	÷	5	1	7	7	7	2	4	2	7	2	÷	÷	9
8	5	6	x	1	1	=	1	x	1	1	8	x	0	8
6	2	2	5	4	1	3	x	−	7	x	2	÷	7	2
3	=	1	x	3	0	1	=	1	x	0	1	6	−	x
2	8	6	−	8	2	3	2	4	5	8	9	2	9	+
8	3	4	−	4	÷	5	3	5	9	0	=	+	7	+
3	4	0	=	6	4	8	7	5	−	1	0	3	0	x
0	2	1	1	x	1	=	1	6	x	9	8	0	÷	4
1	x	−	−	2	1	−	x	2	4	x	9	÷	5	÷
4	+	5	5	x	8	1	5	4	1	1	0	8	0	2
0	1	5	7	1	=	9	0	=	6	=	6	+	2	3
5	8	9	3	6	÷	6	8	1	1	9	6	5	+	7

PAGE 5

6	+	0	6	+	3	8	3	7	6	7	3	2	+	4
9	3	9	1	x	2	=	2	=	8	3	x	2	=	6
9	9	1	=	4	x	4	9	2	x	4	1	3	2	6
0	5	x	2	=	1	0	+	3	÷	2	÷	÷	8	3
3	÷	+	−	+	3	2	5	7	−	=	+	9	4	+
x	8	+	1	4	x	=	2	2	0	2	7	9	4	2
9	3	1	2	0	6	2	1	0	x	x	7	3	x	2
6	x	3	8	0	4	x	−	9	6	2	8	1	÷	=
÷	8	4	4	4	+	0	−	1	÷	1	x	5	4	2
5	5	1	8	÷	2	1	8	0	5	7	2	2	=	x
+	0	=	=	9	÷	1	9	+	6	1	=	6	2	1
6	5	2	2	2	7	2	=	9	x	7	1	3	x	1
x	9	x	x	÷	x	4	3	2	+	÷	6	x	2	5
2	÷	7	4	6	3	9	=	5	x	9	x	6	3	+
9	7	−	3	+	6	2	−	5	6	6	3	6	x	3

PAGE 6

7	9	2	0	5	6	2	x	0	9	2	0	x	2	÷
3	8	x	5	=	4	0	6	2	x	÷	2	5	2	−
7	3	9	0	5	9	1	5	x	4	0	2	x	6	−
4	+	5	2	4	1	5	1	−	0	6	−	x	8	4
1	6	x	9	2	4	7	÷	x	8	8	5	6	4	2
x	÷	+	−	=	8	2	1	3	5	7	9	−	−	4
5	6	1	5	1	4	3	x	2	0	=	1	8	5	9
÷	1	x	8	4	8	8	+	0	x	4	5	5	0	7
5	9	=	3	1	7	2	3	+	1	5	2	5	6	5
2	6	7	5	x	4	3	9	0	2	7	=	5	8	6
=	+	0	5	x	8	4	2	x	−	5	2	6	+	1
5	4	=	7	0	3	2	5	9	x	÷	9	8	0	x
x	3	3	5	6	8	=	2	0	3	2	2	4	8	5
5	2	8	5	6	1	3	1	6	x	5	=	3	0	=
5	+	6	9	0	6	0	2	=	5	x	4	7	4	5

PAGE 7

0	+	8	0	x	6	1	4	7	0	4	÷	1	8	9
6	7	9	3	3	2	6	7	5	4	7	−	0	8	−
+	1	=	−	6	=	3	=	8	7	0	−	9	2	8
6	6	0	0	6	x	0	1	1	=	0	1	x	1	1
6	5	4	5	1	1	1	1	7	1	x	6	1	2	6
−	2	+	1	x	x	3	0	x	8	1	4	+	0	−
3	x	1	5	2	2	7	9	=	3	7	4	8	9	9
4	1	1	4	÷	x	0	÷	x	6	+	9	3	=	1
2	0	5	2	2	6	1	8	x	1	0	=	8	0	+
−	=	1	9	6	8	=	0	3	6	3	2	7	1	5
9	2	6	3	5	7	0	0	=	1	3	÷	+	x	9
2	0	8	4	0	0	1	=	0	1	x	0	1	9	3
5	2	5	3	9	9	x	0	x	1	2	÷	5	9	0
x	7	6	4	3	x	1	3	4	x	1	0	=	4	0
8	x	7	−	1	−	3	1	2	+	1	0	5	5	4

PAGE 8

4	8	6	7	÷	1	+	7	+	4	8	0	4	÷	7
2	7	6	−	x	8	3	÷	6	x	1	=	6	8	6
4	x	2	=	8	1	3	+	2	4	2	1	+	+	5
÷	0	1	9	1	3	0	4	3	8	0	5	7	2	x
x	5	1	0	9	5	3	=	7	x	5	=	3	5	6
+	6	0	9	x	0	6	7	7	5	6	3	4	0	−
+	0	x	2	3	2	0	9	5	0	−	6	3	x	3
0	2	1	+	7	3	=	=	7	÷	8	8	x	3	5
5	4	0	−	=	4	5	2	3	4	x	+	1	7	x
3	9	=	0	6	x	2	0	0	9	2	9	=	7	1
9	+	1	÷	1	5	5	0	1	x	=	3	3	4	=
7	x	0	1	0	=	0	7	7	9	1	4	1	4	5
3	6	0	2	1	2	8	0	4	5	6	4	2	8	6
8	7	2	2	÷	0	4	8	0	2	3	2	2	4	8
4	8	8	3	8	5	9	x	0	0	8	0	+	6	1

PAGE 9

x	5	5	9	7	0	0	6	+	1	6	5	9	0	x
1	0	0	5	6	9	0	4	7	=	x	9	8	4	0
−	0	5	2	=	1	x	2	2	+	4	0	1	5	8
5	x	1	0	=	5	0	x	8	1	=	2	x	9	+
÷	1	1	0	9	−	3	6	÷	9	5	9	5	1	4
4	÷	5	1	5	4	0	−	x	x	5	4	x	−	2
x	9	8	1	2	0	−	5	5	5	2	8	2	4	3
8	3	6	=	2	−	−	÷	9	5	=	x	=	8	0
9	−	÷	0	5	x	x	−	x	2	6	3	1	2	4
x	4	+	1	7	x	1	+	6	8	6	7	0	1	=
1	2	0	x	7	3	5	0	−	3	8	x	+	=	0
0	0	6	1	8	4	1	÷	=	1	0	5	8	1	1
=	4	8	1	0	1	−	2	x	1	−	2	6	x	x
9	3	7	5	2	=	5	x	5	x	2	0	4	2	4
0	+	4	5	3	+	0	1	5	0	9	0	2	1	2

Solutions

PAGE 10

3	÷	1	=	3	2	x	9	2	7	–	4	+	÷	0
x	4	–	–	8	÷	x	6	x	÷	8	–	4	8	1
4	8	3	4	+	1	8	2	x	0	3	÷	–	1	0
1	6	–	x	÷	=	÷	+	5	0	–	8	0	0	6
÷	2	3	4	6	2	3	=	÷	–	3	5	6	8	1
+	x	9	x	5	8	1	4	8	+	÷	5	8	8	7
8	÷	÷	4	–	÷	2	8	0	4	9	7	4	÷	+
8	5	8	2	5	1	6	0	3	2	1	8	–	1	–
8	0	5	1	=	+	6	1	8	6	÷	x	–	=	–
4	9	6	1	0	x	÷	5	0	0	1	2	9	8	4
–	2	÷	÷	6	1	6	0	5	÷	=	4	4	9	7
÷	2	6	8	4	3	÷	1	+	+	1	=	3	3	÷
1	1	÷	1	=	1	1	5	9	÷	1	=	9	1	1
x	2	1	x	6	9	=	9	5	÷	6	2	1	x	=
2	3	4	0	÷	x	6	5	4	5	4	2	÷	0	7

PAGE 11

÷	9	8	3	5	4	÷	6	9	3	6	÷	2	=	3
1	x	7	+	=	3	÷	3	1	4	–	0	6	2	÷
2	8	1	2	8	x	3	9	÷	4	1	x	0	4	5
÷	1	÷	1	0	4	+	3	7	=	÷	÷	9	+	x
2	8	7	2	9	+	0	x	2	4	÷	2	=	1	2
=	2	8	2	=	4	4	÷	7	–	–	0	=	8	x
6	2	+	3	4	9	0	4	5	1	5	1	÷	7	7
0	÷	5	2	0	2	5	9	x	8	0	8	+	0	÷
6	2	4	7	4	5	6	8	–	x	4	x	9	4	3
2	=	x	6	=	9	–	8	7	9	x	5	3	–	4
2	1	6	2	2	–	=	2	2	–	–	÷	3	–	9
÷	1	÷	=	+	2	3	2	÷	2	=	1	6	+	3
–	0	2	7	÷	4	7	–	–	8	4	5	8	–	8
1	÷	9	6	÷	3	1	7	8	x	6	3	1	0	0
4	9	1	÷	x	2	–	÷	4	9	6	8	9	5	0

PAGE 12

1	–	3	+	+	–	–	9	2	3	÷	1	3	x	0
0	1	8	x	4	4	5	0	÷	5	=	1	0	2	–
÷	1	+	–	3	1	5	6	0	3	7	2	8	5	8
5	7	4	1	–	+	4	9	1	7	6	÷	6	÷	4
=	0	6	1	+	4	3	4	=	2	9	=	7	5	x
2	4	–	9	1	5	+	5	0	7	5	3	4	=	0
–	3	x	8	–	÷	÷	2	0	÷	5	=	4	5	x
–	÷	+	+	4	5	–	4	0	x	5	+	7	2	÷
5	2	x	2	3	=	5	3	x	–	4	=	2	4	5
1	÷	1	x	3	9	1	5	÷	5	=	3	8	7	+
x	5	5	÷	5	=	1	1	9	1	2	8	4	9	1
x	5	÷	=	1	8	6	0	÷	5	=	1	2	6	–
x	7	x	4	1	2	÷	9	x	x	1	2	0	4	6
8	3	9	2	1	÷	x	7	9	5	x	2	3	0	3
2	0	0	8	4	4	5	6	3	+	2	0	x	8	x

PAGE 13

9	2	1	6	7	0	0	8	7	6	9	+	3	x	0
4	7	4	÷	0	9	8	5	=	÷	–	7	8	6	9
2	5	5	3	–	6	8	0	8	2	2	0	4	–	0
÷	3	4	+	1	5	1	4	÷	1	–	÷	x	5	÷
3	9	5	1	–	÷	=	1	3	1	6	1	5	0	1
+	5	+	–	0	0	3	5	0	÷	0	0	9	÷	0
1	4	8	6	1	6	4	1	–	÷	5	=	+	1	=
1	2	0	÷	1	0	=	1	2	1	1	7	8	0	9
7	7	0	6	0	0	8	7	+	1	–	0	–	=	3
÷	4	3	6	1	0	÷	1	0	=	1	5	=	5	+
8	3	0	÷	1	0	=	3	7	x	9	9	1	1	9
–	2	0	÷	1	0	=	2	8	÷	5	+	5	7	1
3	0	4	6	÷	7	x	5	0	9	5	–	1	–	6
1	x	–	4	3	+	6	5	–	5	÷	0	8	3	0
1	9	+	0	8	7	9	8	1	+	8	–	–	÷	1

PAGE 14

1	6	1	5	2	+	9	÷	2	1	5	+	8	6	5
2	3	2	–	1	x	6	5	x	–	7	3	1	6	÷
0	6	6	9	8	3	=	0	–	2	0	÷	5	=	4
÷	5	8	7	9	1	3	8	–	4	9	2	x	1	5
1	6	8	+	÷	x	+	2	9	0	÷	4	5	3	3
0	x	7	5	0	÷	5	=	1	0	–	–	÷	9	0
=	9	8	+	4	9	8	1	2	8	8	9	9	x	3
1	2	0	÷	2	=	1	0	3	0	÷	5	=	6	3
2	2	2	=	0	=	+	x	9	4	6	8	6	3	0
1	6	1	1	5	2	5	5	2	÷	=	x	5	6	÷
+	÷	÷	÷	8	1	5	÷	8	1	9	7	1	2	1
2	0	5	÷	+	3	1	+	÷	9	5	÷	9	2	0
8	5	3	1	3	2	6	8	4	6	–	3	4	6	=
6	–	6	–	1	x	–	1	3	7	6	÷	8	9	3
2	4	÷	2	=	1	2	7	+	9	7	0	6	+	2

PAGE 15

1	+	–	5	+	0	+	6	+	–	6	3	7	9	3
4	5	5	0	2	5	÷	1	+	0	+	3	3	6	÷
+	0	+	0	2	0	+	0	0	–	4	4	6	x	x
x	3	–	–	÷	5	9	÷	+	7	5	–	÷	+	7
7	3	6	4	0	1	+	1	+	÷	÷	7	5	8	1
6	9	3	1	x	6	0	0	3	5	5	4	–	2	1
7	÷	4	3	5	÷	5	=	7	÷	=	+	6	9	0
4	1	1	÷	1	=	1	1	5	3	9	3	–	4	6
9	3	4	8	1	1	0	÷	1	0	=	1	1	2	÷
3	–	0	÷	x	2	x	1	2	2	6	x	9	8	4
7	5	÷	÷	2	+	÷	3	6	6	9	2	4	8	6
4	0	4	÷	0	=	8	2	1	9	8	9	–	÷	÷
1	0	÷	5	=	2	7	6	=	3	4	2	9	2	2
7	x	x	1	8	÷	2	=	9	6	8	8	6	=	=
x	7	0	+	7	1	7	5	1	8	4	–	–	4	3

PAGE 16

7	x	3	=	2	1	8	1	4	0	6	0	6	7	1
3	8	1	÷	0	0	6	2	2	4	x	3	=	1	2
9	÷	5	3	4	2	0	9	+	6	x	÷	5	2	9
+	x	3	÷	1	1	–	0	=	3	1	4	x	x	4
7	1	4	7	1	6	3	3	=	÷	8	÷	–	3	2
x	7	3	9	x	=	x	9	–	4	9	0	8	=	7
7	+	6	2	3	2	x	x	2	x	1	8	÷	3	+
÷	3	1	x	=	3	3	=	3	0	–	1	÷	6	1
4	3	0	2	3	–	3	=	+	x	÷	=	3	÷	x
2	1	–	÷	3	x	2	3	3	x	8	3	7	9	4
9	3	2	÷	8	7	÷	+	9	x	x	x	x	x	÷
9	9	9	–	2	8	2	3	4	5	1	6	5	3	7
7	5	7	9	8	4	4	x	9	5	9	+	+	0	–
÷	8	+	4	+	9	–	5	3	3	5	6	5	4	2
2	–	5	5	1	=	3	x	5	6	+	1	+	1	4

PAGE 17

1	5	4	x	+	2	5	4	2	x	0	4	3	2	7
3	0	8	÷	4	7	4	1	2	x	4	=	4	8	8
6	0	x	2	1	=	4	x	3	=	1	7	5	4	+
÷	x	2	4	1	6	1	5	4	x	2	–	9	÷	x
5	9	5	x	=	4	8	x	4	9	x	4	=	3	6
÷	3	4	x	9	4	1	9	÷	–	4	5	7	4	8
–	=	9	+	4	1	0	3	x	x	–	3	2	7	9
4	+	6	2	8	=	+	–	4	–	7	=	–	x	8
6	6	1	1	4	2	2	=	x	÷	4	÷	–	4	6
x	4	3	x	8	8	1	0	–	x	3	2	+	=	4
÷	6	2	3	÷	6	7	x	6	1	–	3	x	2	7
x	7	x	÷	–	x	9	0	9	9	6	=	2	8	2
6	2	4	–	7	1	9	7	2	4	8	4	4	x	3
3	3	=	+	8	+	4	0	1	7	7	x	x	÷	2
9	1	8	0	3	5	–	x	1	–	5	8	1	3	7

PAGE 18

9	7	x	4	x	0	6	x	x	2	7	2	1	8	0
2	0	1	6	5	1	0	4	÷	9	6	5	1	4	6
7	3	0	8	x	4	=	3	2	1	9	3	6	1	3
0	6	1	3	4	4	8	8	–	3	6	3	1	x	3
x	x	=	6	0	–	4	2	8	2	2	2	3	2	÷
÷	3	8	x	3	=	2	4	x	+	x	=	x	3	7
0	=	1	+	x	3	x	÷	8	4	9	x	3	+	2
3	1	2	÷	4	6	3	–	=	1	9	–	5	4	7
=	8	x	4	=	6	0	4	4	–	0	x	1	x	+
3	6	3	4	1	1	8	3	5	5	÷	+	7	6	8
x	7	=	=	2	5	–	1	6	3	1	4	7	5	5
0	7	3	4	3	2	8	÷	0	4	=	4	x	0	1
1	1	6	x	x	7	8	6	x	7	7	2	9	2	7
9	–	0	1	7	–	2	4	0	2	=	4	x	5	5
–	1	x	1	0	x	2	4	6	9	7	8	3	x	8

Solutions

PAGE 19

9	−	+	0	7	x	6	+	4	2	=	4	x	6	8
5	4	−	6	6	4	4	5	0	2	6	+	÷	4	4
4	4	x	3	=	1	2	+	3	3	0	2	−	6	+
3	3	=	3	x	1	1	8	=	0	3	8	+	9	÷
1	3	3	÷	7	1	6	4	2	9	−	x	1	x	7
2	4	9	8	5	÷	x	5	9	=	1	2	x	3	÷
=	5	5	x	8	9	9	1	9	3	4	5	6	=	+
3	3	1	8	5	9	8	=	÷	−	5	x	7	2	x
x	−	−	÷	=	0	8	3	5	÷	3	9	7	7	7
7	8	4	0	+	4	4	x	4	7	6	÷	4	−	0
÷	3	4	=	5	3	x	5	5	6	7	1	÷	6	4
0	8	÷	6	4	2	4	2	2	=	1	x	4	6	2
x	7	2	8	5	x	=	+	9	3	+	0	÷	÷	−
x	9	7	÷	5	÷	1	4	9	x	+	7	6	−	0
8	−	+	2	+	2	6	9	9	2	9	+	4	0	+

PAGE 20

1	x	8	5	x	÷	9	−	1	+	6	4	0	1	4
0	+	−	3	x	7	6	8	7	7	4	−	9	2	−
6	−	8	4	÷	÷	6	x	x	1	2	4	0	÷	x
3	÷	8	9	9	4	+	9	1	1	+	8	7	3	5
7	9	6	3	0	−	0	1	=	5	6	2	8	=	4
7	1	÷	÷	÷	+	=	3	4	2	1	9	÷	4	9
6	3	3	4	8	3	÷	1	1	1	9	x	5	0	÷
1	8	=	2	÷	3	9	=	÷	1	5	÷	3	=	5
6	5	2	3	0	÷	3	=	1	0	8	6	÷	7	2
1	0	3	8	2	÷	8	5	0	÷	3	6	2	2	0
8	5	5	5	6	1	3	5	9	÷	9	0	3	7	5
÷	0	4	3	x	7	÷	1	4	x	3	2	÷	÷	+
3	3	+	6	4	2	8	3	+	0	3	7	8	3	7
=	÷	6	3	9	5	+	x	=	2	4	÷	3	=	8
6	+	x	0	9	÷	3	=	3	7	0	8	0	9	3

PAGE 21

6	3	3	−	1	+	1	x	−	4	9	8	5	4	0
1	4	−	4	4	7	−	8	5	x	1	+	7	−	3
2	0	4	4	9	1	x	0	0	9	1	0	4	5	2
÷	÷	1	x	÷	9	1	2	=	÷	6	4	6	+	÷
4	4	3	6	−	9	0	4	÷	8	÷	8	5	x	4
=	=	7	÷	8	8	÷	3	1	−	4	÷	−	2	=
3	1	0	1	0	6	+	4	9	2	=	4	4	0	8
5	0	9	1	3	8	4	+	1	6	4	=	4	÷	+
x	+	6	+	+	6	8	2	4	3	0	1	÷	4	2
3	+	5	7	2	x	7	6	÷	÷	x	2	4	=	−
1	9	9	=	6	+	5	4	x	6	4	9	=	5	8
x	÷	4	x	1	+	÷	8	5	5	x	=	1	x	x
5	÷	8	6	2	8	8	9	x	7	1	5	1	9	4
8	+	9	4	−	3	0	3	7	4	7	+	2	7	x
2	8	÷	4	=	7	2	4	÷	4	=	6	7	5	0

PAGE 22

1	2	÷	4	=	3	6	5	5	7	3	9	3	1	+
0	6	2	4	2	2	−	−	6	÷	x	4	+	8	8
2	+	6	5	3	÷	4	6	5	0	x	−	÷	÷	−
8	÷	4	=	2	6	=	÷	+	2	3	+	x	3	1
3	8	1	−	0	4	4	1	3	+	4	4	9	=	7
9	x	5	0	÷	7	1	8	9	=	6	÷	1	6	1
8	2	6	4	1	=	=	8	+	6	8	4	4	÷	÷
x	x	2	x	4	4	7	5	3	+	6	−	9	=	2
6	7	9	÷	÷	5	x	2	x	x	4	5	3	8	1
−	÷	4	2	7	4	÷	7	4	7	−	+	0	1	÷
4	4	3	−	3	−	6	7	5	+	2	4	÷	4	3
9	6	0	=	7	8	4	7	x	÷	0	1	3	6	=
5	2	7	6	2	1	6	4	8	9	6	÷	=	4	7
+	7	0	9	÷	3	=	3	4	2	4	3	1	÷	2
7	5	7	9	3	8	0	9	x	8	5	÷	0	x	8

PAGE 23

7	3	÷	8	−	1	2	8	÷	4	=	7	1	8	2
7	4	8	÷	4	=	1	2	2	x	÷	4	6	5	5
9	0	0	9	x	5	4	7	7	1	0	8	÷	6	0
5	4	2	3	=	6	0	0	1	−	−	6	4	3	1
x	+	2	4	8	1	5	7	÷	6	2	x	=	÷	+
−	+	÷	3	x	−	9	x	5	4	6	2	4	3	4
4	0	6	+	7	−	3	0	6	÷	=	9	1	=	−
2	1	0	3	2	8	x	6	1	3	−	1	8	1	9
7	7	2	6	3	9	5	6	÷	2	1	2	0	=	1
7	9	5	6	=	÷	0	9	1	3	6	÷	4	5	2
1	x	+	3	6	1	3	4	8	÷	=	÷	4	÷	÷
÷	7	÷	−	9	−	9	=	7	5	6	1	7	÷	3
5	7	1	5	÷	3	=	5	1	3	+	7	2	÷	=
2	0	3	−	−	9	÷	4	1	1	+	−	7	+	4
6	9	2	7	+	7	x	4	6	2	9	8	4	+	3

PAGE 24

8	0	+	7	−	8	7	0	3	=	6	x	5	−	2
÷	7	7	4	4	1	0	8	2	3	2	8	5	4	8
6	0	−	7	4	2	1	4	−	7	0	x	0	2	1
7	8	+	+	2	8	1	=	+	9	=	x	0	6	3
9	4	−	3	0	0	x	6	1	7	3	6	−	÷	9
5	x	0	5	4	8	6	x	2	3	7	÷	x	÷	x
6	6	−	9	7	÷	=	8	5	÷	5	9	1	2	2
4	=	3	8	1	9	6	7	8	1	4	1	8	2	1
÷	2	3	−	x	1	6	9	2	3	3	1	0	1	7
0	4	÷	6	0	3	2	−	−	3	−	0	9	=	2
2	0	=	+	=	x	1	1	4	x	0	x	5	6	4
÷	5	÷	6	8	2	x	9	6	8	2	6	−	x	=
4	÷	x	8	1	=	6	x	3	1	4	=	0	2	6
6	6	5	0	x	÷	=	7	0	1	7	6	1	−	x
6	4	8	6	x	8	6	3	÷	÷	7	0	7	0	7

PAGE 25

2	2	1	0	2	−	5	9	2	4	1	5	1	8	1
9	7	+	+	4	1	+	−	6	1	3	3	4	6	2
8	+	÷	2	=	4	5	8	x	8	6	x	3	1	x
1	4	+	5	7	x	1	7	6	6	=	7	9	5	7
0	7	5	7	x	8	=	4	5	1	7	=	6	x	=
x	0	÷	−	6	7	5	=	8	6	x	2	2	+	8
7	9	4	2	7	1	7	0	7	+	9	1	+	2	4
=	1	4	0	7	x	8	2	x	7	=	1	4	6	5
7	4	2	0	8	9	4	=	7	x	7	9	8	5	0
0	÷	÷	+	4	1	5	9	0	7	2	0	2	x	4
7	+	÷	x	8	6	−	1	−	0	5	1	=	7	9
8	3	x	9	+	−	7	x	÷	0	4	3	7	=	1
2	3	0	8	9	6	1	7	0	4	6	4	x	3	3
7	9	7	4	−	8	7	=	8	3	4	6	4	5	9
3	2	2	1	5	÷	x	7	x	÷	1	−	9	2	6

PAGE 26

2	0	6	=	6	x	0	1	5	2	9	8	÷	8	6
0	−	2	7	=	6	x	2	1	0	−	7	2	x	4
−	4	+	2	5	6	8	2	4	+	4	4	x	+	2
5	5	3	6	−	÷	7	3	9	x	1	8	1	−	÷
1	8	−	9	÷	4	1	1	x	1	6	−	x	3	x
÷	4	4	8	=	7	x	2	1	6	2	6	x	6	1
6	3	=	6	x	6	+	x	6	5	=	7	0	0	5
3	5	2	8	7	+	8	0	1	6	3	1	x	1	3
x	7	3	1	7	÷	2	2	6	2	3	9	8	3	−
7	x	9	7	=	9	+	6	6	=	6	x	1	2	0
=	6	6	4	7	÷	2	−	x	5	3	+	5	9	0
2	=	3	÷	x	+	÷	x	8	0	=	1	4	0	7
1	4	2	0	1	1	x	÷	3	4	x	7	=	2	8
2	2	8	6	1	2	x	−	3	9	5	3	x	6	÷
0	7	=	7	x	0	1	1	−	1	8	+	x	8	2

PAGE 27

x	5	3	1	1	6	−	5	5	+	8	÷	÷	÷	4
1	1	x	6	=	6	6	+	8	0	8	7	0	x	÷
7	=	7	x	1	9	x	6	=	5	4	3	6	x	−
8	0	÷	1	9	5	+	−	5	1	6	=	7	3	4
3	7	3	6	−	7	2	+	5	9	2	6	9	−	4
−	8	6	8	−	8	0	x	5	4	7	2	8	+	9
x	4	1	9	4	3	4	4	3	+	6	÷	0	7	4
x	9	8	8	x	5	−	=	0	÷	2	÷	3	6	=
4	1	5	4	−	x	3	8	6	÷	9	4	=	2	7
2	2	1	÷	4	4	1	=	7	x	2	8	6	÷	x
1	2	4	=	7	x	6	9	7	8	8	7	x	+	7
=	−	3	6	7	−	−	1	+	x	3	5	5	2	7
6	3	6	x	9	−	÷	+	5	1	5	2	7	0	5
x	7	+	8	1	2	4	9	9	0	0	5	x	7	x
2	9	x	7	=	6	3	÷	0	6	5	6	4	8	4

Solutions

PAGE 28

−	9	−	x	6	1	−	3	2	8	8	1	2	−	x
−	+	5	8	0	3	1	1	−	1	=	2	4	x	3
6	+	0	7	5	0	4	8	÷	6	=	8	÷	4	6
2	7	6	9	4	4	5	5	÷	8	0	0	6	−	÷
0	1	3	1	7	0	2	6	3	3	x	4	=	6	6
7	0	−	x	2	5	÷	0	6	x	x	1	4	7	=
3	1	7	2	x	÷	8	÷	7	÷	7	2	x	2	6
5	2	x	1	÷	7	6	6	÷	1	6	3	4	÷	−
5	3	3	8	3	8	4	=	6	x	3	=	8	6	8
2	0	÷	÷	2	−	5	1	2	9	1	1	1	=	3
3	8	1	6	7	+	4	0	−	1	8	−	5	1	+
−	9	9	=	0	5	÷	9	5	7	0	5	1	2	9
0	7	6	3	2	8	6	2	1	4	2	÷	6	=	7
3	x	−	+	2	÷	=	+	8	6	÷	3	−	7	7
3	0	÷	6	=	5	9	+	3	1	6	3	5	÷	−

PAGE 29

x	3	÷	9	6	1	5	2	x	+	5	7	7	9	0
4	4	0	2	=	3	÷	2	6	−	3	6	9	9	8
2	1	÷	7	=	3	4	9	÷	7	=	7	−	2	7
−	7	÷	+	8	4	4	÷	7	1	−	6	6	3	5
8	7	1	+	1	4	x	2	0	7	4	7	5	0	7
9	÷	3	÷	1	−	÷	5	÷	7	4	÷	0	2	3
−	7	÷	4	6	2	=	7	7	7	6	5	7	8	2
6	=	x	4	7	7	0	0	=	5	=	8	3	=	−
3	1	9	4	÷	1	÷	6	1	1	1	6	2	0	2
÷	1	6	5	9	9	7	2	0	6	2	+	4	3	4
7	3	3	8	1	9	5	6	÷	7	=	8	÷	+	−
=	+	5	2	+	÷	1	9	+	5	4	−	1	8	7
9	8	+	3	7	4	2	8	÷	7	=	4	7	5	3
4	3	−	9	4	2	8	÷	1	4	9	0	3	+	+
9	7	4	4	7	÷	7	2	0	5	9	1	8	4	÷

PAGE 30

3	7	÷	9	÷	5	5	0	8	5	3	2	+	0	9
6	0	1	0	0	1	2	÷	6	=	2	1	+	+	9
÷	3	÷	÷	5	5	−	3	7	0	8	1	1	5	7
6	7	7	6	0	0	6	+	5	0	3	7	x	4	0
=	6	3	7	=	÷	3	÷	0	9	9	6	8	1	÷
6	1	8	4	x	5	8	1	4	2	x	−	6	x	7
+	4	÷	9	7	9	=	1	4	÷	7	=	2	4	=
3	x	6	4	=	6	9	1	4	6	1	1	x	8	1
4	6	−	7	÷	2	1	x	4	=	9	2	x	x	0
7	0	÷	0	7	x	4	=	7	+	9	1	4	5	÷
7	3	6	−	8	0	6	÷	1	3	3	÷	−	÷	÷
6	1	−	2	8	÷	7	=	4	4	9	÷	7	=	7
+	8	+	+	4	2	÷	6	=	7	4	0	6	5	7
÷	4	5	2	3	5	5	8	0	÷	+	6	0	9	3
6	3	+	6	+	÷	9	8	5	1	3	+	1	7	8

PAGE 31

6	8	4	÷	7	=	1	2	x	3	6	0	4	2	1
6	x	3	7	6	÷	5	7	−	2	x	7	3	−	8
÷	1	5	2	÷	x	÷	+	6	1	x	2	3	+	÷
6	8	3	6	7	+	7	5	0	÷	x	÷	4	5	5
=	÷	+	1	÷	4	5	4	1	9	+	6	−	2	−
1	6	8	−	3	7	8	1	9	2	4	=	7	÷	+
1	=	÷	6	0	x	=	=	7	8	x	1	5	8	8
−	3	4	4	0	7	6	8	−	7	4	2	+	3	5
4	3	÷	3	÷	÷	0	x	5	+	4	9	8	=	3
2	7	9	7	4	+	x	9	÷	9	+	4	7	2	0
÷	7	7	5	1	5	6	6	3	÷	6	÷	8	1	7
7	5	−	=	1	6	1	9	1	2	5	x	+	6	7
=	8	6	4	8	÷	6	=	8	3	3	x	+	0	9
6	÷	8	4	−	5	÷	÷	2	÷	7	x	9	2	1
6	5	1	6	−	0	6	2	1	÷	7	=	3	7	7

PAGE 32

4	0	8	0	1	0	9	0	1	8	2	0	4	9	7
+	0	=	−	7	3	5	÷	2	9	−	5	8	x	8
2	5	8	7	4	7	9	2	x	6	3	4	3	6	9
9	6	x	0	0	7	6	4	9	8	5	−	5	5	9
2	8	1	0	2	x	8	4	1	9	3	=	x	8	8
3	6	8	9	8	6	−	3	5	−	÷	8	8	−	+
=	+	3	=	+	3	5	8	2	1	=	−	5	x	9
8	3	4	1	6	1	4	5	8	4	2	6	÷	3	7
x	8	0	1	9	3	6	÷	0	8	=	8	x	0	1
4	2	+	2	=	8	=	0	6	4	7	+	2	+	1
6	7	÷	5	8	3	8	6	5	3	9	÷	5	5	9
4	=	5	4	x	3	x	8	=	2	4	4	9	−	7
8	8	x	4	2	2	8	0	7	÷	3	7	8	9	2
4	x	+	3	1	8	2	x	8	=	1	6	0	6	1
x	9	+	6	9	9	8	8	=	8	x	1	1	5	+

PAGE 33

x	1	0	x	9	=	9	0	0	3	x	2	2	9	1
2	2	÷	0	5	÷	5	−	8	9	4	9	0	÷	8
6	÷	−	2	1	9	7	3	3	7	7	−	7	6	0
6	1	5	4	=	9	x	5	1	6	1	6	7	1	1
x	4	4	9	2	+	+	÷	1	7	÷	8	3	5	=
9	−	+	8	8	7	8	8	4	7	8	1	2	9	9
3	7	+	7	3	6	=	7	7	1	−	1	5	9	x
−	x	6	2	3	9	4	9	÷	−	7	x	4	2	2
8	9	8	x	x	9	5	4	x	2	1	4	6	2	1
9	=	2	9	+	+	=	x	=	8	9	5	1	0	5
8	6	1	=	8	6	9	9	−	1	8	x	−	3	3
1	3	x	1	3	6	x	=	9	9	=	9	x	1	1
÷	7	9	8	+	3	6	3	7	−	2	2	9	3	÷
1	÷	=	5	4	−	2	6	x	2	÷	0	9	3	3
7	+	9	6	1	3	7	5	0	7	6	6	+	9	−

PAGE 34

0	0	0	÷	4	x	9	=	3	6	0	6	6	6	−
5	5	x	÷	1	9	÷	9	8	+	2	9	5	3	3
0	1	1	x	8	=	8	8	6	x	=	3	x	7	+
1	0	÷	2	−	÷	1	3	3	8	x	÷	8	1	8
0	−	x	+	9	4	2	5	x	9	5	+	=	2	3
x	8	−	5	x	9	2	2	=	2	3	2	4	3	4
9	9	8	5	7	0	1	2	9	8	3	0	0	7	7
=	3	5	7	4	9	7	x	4	9	9	=	8	7	x
9	6	6	3	5	÷	1	8	÷	6	=	5	8	x	7
0	÷	1	8	÷	x	7	=	÷	8	=	9	4	x	5
9	4	7	1	4	7	x	1	0	5	7	8	x	x	4
x	6	7	=	1	−	5	6	x	3	3	1	x	1	4
8	7	x	9	9	0	9	5	2	9	1	4	4	8	1
÷	x	3	x	6	÷	4	x	x	0	=	0	0	1	÷
3	−	2	2	÷	9	−	+	5	−	1	9	5	÷	2

PAGE 35

4	x	÷	9	x	÷	2	÷	+	9	9	3	2	6	8
6	6	5	x	6	−	1	9	−	x	÷	x	0	5	−
8	÷	9	9	5	x	9	=	4	5	÷	7	1	0	÷
x	+	+	=	9	÷	3	7	+	3	+	3	6	6	0
−	x	5	8	÷	−	x	x	4	2	=	8	x	3	8
2	−	÷	1	3	2	6	x	÷	8	9	÷	÷	9	=
4	4	÷	+	8	6	9	+	x	8	4	3	x	x	8
7	x	0	÷	0	8	x	9	=	7	2	=	÷	7	x
0	1	3	0	1	7	5	3	6	2	5	8	8	5	0
4	−	÷	÷	=	x	7	÷	5	x	0	−	+	x	1
1	0	2	6	9	9	1	x	6	x	9	=	5	4	6
x	x	4	2	x	=	7	1	8	3	8	+	5	8	3
8	8	÷	+	2	6	4	x	8	=	3	2	1	3	8
=	2	0	÷	1	3	6	1	1	6	5	6	−	÷	0
8	8	9	2	9	x	4	−	3	0	+	6	2	3	6

PAGE 36

1	6	÷	8	=	2	9	8	8	1	+	9	7	8	÷
3	9	3	9	4	5	9	7	=	÷	÷	x	6	8	1
4	2	3	3	2	9	3	8	8	÷	8	=	1	1	+
5	1	÷	4	7	+	÷	+	5	8	3	+	−	4	1
9	6	6	8	1	8	x	5	0	9	0	7	6	0	8
6	4	÷	7	=	5	÷	+	9	x	9	8	7	=	8
÷	0	8	8	6	4	x	6	6	4	1	0	8	4	4
8	÷	7	3	=	3	5	4	÷	÷	7	÷	1	8	3
=	8	3	1	=	7	8	x	+	÷	4	8	2	÷	9
1	=	4	8	+	−	5	4	5	6	+	=	−	8	8
2	5	÷	9	7	2	÷	8	=	9	1	1	8	=	1
÷	4	5	5	÷	7	7	5	+	2	3	0	8	6	x
2	8	0	4	7	7	4	6	x	9	6	x	2	x	+
1	0	5	7	3	7	−	÷	4	5	9	x	÷	8	6
4	1	0	0	2	2	x	+	÷	÷	+	+	8	8	5

Solutions

PAGE 37

2	−	8	−	6	−	4	3	1	x	0	÷	0	5	x
7	7	÷	9	0	4	−	1	8	÷	9	=	2	÷	3
÷	4	9	4	9	3	=	1	5	6	3	÷	9	=	7
9	3	−	+	−	9	5	x	4	+	÷	9	4	x	2
=	x	9	4	÷	1	4	9	÷	3	6	÷	9	=	4
3	−	0	9	1	÷	1	5	9	2	2	8	0	−	3
4	÷	9	7	−	−	6	+	=	6	8	1	8	5	2
5	5	7	7	4	0	÷	9	6	2	=	÷	2	2	7
7	÷	÷	x	0	+	7	7	÷	9	8	9	1	8	4
4	8	+	9	5	8	3	5	÷	6	÷	=	4	5	8
2	−	4	1	=	÷	0	0	9	9	3	9	9	2	+
x	5	0	9	2	5	9	7	÷	÷	4	9	÷	8	+
−	3	÷	2	6	8	5	3	8	6	2	7	9	0	+
2	2	+	x	1	0	8	÷	9	=	1	2	=	8	4
7	÷	5	6	2	6	6	7	1	4	+	6	1	÷	1

PAGE 38

4	3	3	2	7	÷	9	=	3	1	4	−	1	÷	3
5	8	8	÷	2	÷	8	x	−	3	4	3	9	8	2
÷	+	3	1	2	÷	1	0	7	8	+	4	4	+	1
9	4	4	5	7	5	1	1	5	8	+	7	3	6	4
=	8	x	+	3	x	6	9	4	8	x	2	5	7	5
5	x	6	5	÷	7	1	÷	5	÷	0	2	9	5	x
÷	x	2	8	0	÷	8	=	1	0	1	x	0	1	−
9	÷	3	3	2	÷	8	=	4	=	8	÷	8	=	1
7	9	7	6	÷	÷	÷	=	9	x	5	8	6	4	+
2	x	4	3	0	3	9	÷	8	+	4	7	2	3	9
3	−	3	4	7	÷	8	7	0	0	÷	8	4	x	0
÷	x	0	7	6	0	+	8	9	3	9	5	÷	5	0
5	8	3	3	1	÷	x	2	5	5	=	2	8	2	2
8	4	8	÷	8	=	6	9	6	−	6	8	=	0	+
3	x	1	9	9	÷	9	=	1	1	7	8	3	2	÷

PAGE 39

9	0	÷	9	=	1	0	3	2	4	1	6	+	0	x
3	9	÷	+	3	3	5	5	2	5	9	2	5	−	5
2	7	8	9	6	9	1	8	+	4	1	1	5	−	4
0	÷	÷	4	+	7	x	+	6	=	−	5	+	4	−
6	4	÷	8	=	8	4	+	8	1	0	−	0	0	−
6	0	1	9	0	5	4	÷	1	9	2	1	+	3	6
x	5	÷	3	1	3	6	=	+	7	2	÷	8	=	9
2	3	÷	2	4	9	8	x	3	4	−	4	1	+	5
6	3	2	−	+	÷	0	x	3	4	0	7	÷	4	6
8	+	3	2	8	7	8	1	2	2	3	8	9	7	÷
1	3	÷	8	9	8	5	5	=	8	1	3	=	2	8
8	+	÷	0	÷	3	−	8	3	x	3	6	9	÷	=
2	1	x	8	9	1	÷	+	+	7	x	0	x	9	7
2	+	x	8	=	6	0	7	3	9	3	÷	+	=	+
6	7	+	3	1	9	9	1	8	÷	9	=	2	8	8

PAGE 40

8	4	2	2	4	5	7	8	x	3	5	3	7	1	x
3	x	2	4	2	0	x	1	4	−	9	4	9	2	x
9	1	=	3	−	7	−	0	3	−	1	2	1	3	0
7	1	1	x	1	1	=	1	1	2	−	+	−	1	7
0	=	1	+	5	7	9	3	8	+	7	9	0	=	1
8	4	x	4	4	x	5	8	2	÷	6	7	5	1	0
8	4	2	−	1	x	3	4	8	4	5	7	5	1	x
+	9	3	1	2	0	÷	0	+	=	7	=	=	x	1
+	−	=	6	6	=	1	1	x	6	1	1	1	2	1
÷	9	5	1	1	2	1	=	1	1	x	1	1	1	=
9	x	5	9	9	2	÷	x	4	8	7	x	x	÷	1
3	+	+	1	3	x	1	1	=	3	3	7	5	8	1
0	2	0	4	2	−	3	4	5	−	4	7	2	4	0
7	−	6	6	9	9	2	4	4	8	−	÷	4	−	1
3	7	6	−	3	÷	0	7	+	1	7	0	7	+	+

PAGE 41

−	1	0	1	9	4	−	+	3	9	÷	6	x	8	2
1	4	0	4	3	4	8	=	2	1	x	7	9	8	0
+	1	1	4	3	1	9	7	6	x	÷	6	9	8	6
2	1	+	4	x	1	2	=	4	8	2	−	9	1	=
6	x	4	9	7	+	3	4	+	2	8	6	8	6	2
1	1	−	3	9	+	2	6	÷	3	3	0	x	x	1
x	2	1	2	4	=	1	x	8	=	2	9	1	5	x
1	=	3	4	2	5	6	0	2	1	5	−	2	5	5
2	1	÷	1	÷	x	1	1	=	0	5	3	=	6	x
=	3	x	÷	5	=	x	2	9	7	5	−	9	9	6
1	2	5	0	2	3	1	0	3	2	4	÷	6	3	÷
2	+	9	1	2	x	1	2	=	1	4	4	5	7	5
÷	x	x	7	0	2	7	=	2	1	x	6	9	3	7
9	9	x	1	6	0	7	8	+	2	6	6	+	7	4
2	x	x	2	2	5	9	7	0	5	5	8	0	3	4

PAGE 42

8	3	4	6	x	1	1	=	6	6	3	9	−	1	4
2	3	1	=	2	1	x	1	1	9	7	3	3	1	4
+	5	4	9	1	2	9	0	−	x	÷	8	÷	+	1
0	1	1	=	1	1	x	0	1	+	7	5	3	6	=
9	7	7	x	9	+	x	2	−	0	x	2	3	5	2
9	9	3	9	7	÷	=	1	0	1	1	x	9	3	1
÷	x	x	÷	÷	8	7	÷	1	−	−	1	+	−	x
6	5	1	9	4	6	2	=	1	=	x	1	1	9	2
÷	−	0	2	÷	8	5	1	8	9	1	=	2	x	1
7	3	2	2	=	5	=	8	6	x	1	2	=	7	2
8	−	+	8	2	1	+	−	0	5	−	2	1	3	÷
1	7	÷	x	1	5	0	x	3	9	9	1	7	1	9
5	0	8	x	4	8	3	8	3	x	1	2	=	3	6
9	1	1	6	2	7	÷	9	6	6	÷	0	8	3	÷
1	x	1	4	−	8	5	2	3	3	2	5	7	4	4

PAGE 43

4	4	+	2	8	7	9	x	1	1	=	9	9	+	9
÷	9	6	6	2	−	2	x	1	2	=	2	4	−	0
4	8	−	8	−	3	4	x	2	9	+	1	1	6	6
4	9	1	5	x	7	1	4	1	x	0	x	8	1	2
9	4	1	0	x	1	2	=	1	2	0	1	5	3	8
4	6	3	0	8	3	2	÷	1	3	9	2	x	÷	1
2	4	−	6	÷	3	7	=	5	1	÷	=	8	−	4
7	1	1	8	4	=	3	x	9	+	x	1	0	x	4
x	7	1	7	+	1	6	2	1	6	7	2	−	4	=
1	0	÷	3	5	1	+	3	2	2	9	−	1	x	1
1	8	x	8	3	x	+	5	−	5	7	5	4	1	1
=	x	4	−	0	3	5	x	1	2	=	6	0	2	x
7	+	6	8	−	9	8	8	3	3	5	8	0	=	4
7	0	5	0	3	6	9	6	9	x	4	7	7	4	7
1	0	8	2	9	x	4	8	8	=	1	1	x	8	4

PAGE 44

÷	3	x	0	3	9	3	3	÷	1	1	=	3	9	8
7	9	0	4	0	6	÷	4	9	2	3	1	3	2	0
7	5	1	7	−	4	6	1	9	1	4	1	x	2	0
÷	1	9	−	÷	6	x	÷	÷	5	1	2	4	÷	4
1	1	9	4	÷	1	÷	9	1	=	3	9	0	1	4
1	0	2	0	7	3	8	8	1	1	3	1	5	1	÷
=	÷	+	−	1	4	7	1	=	÷	=	3	5	=	1
7	1	5	÷	+	9	÷	÷	9	0	1	6	÷	2	1
8	1	6	1	5	1	+	5	2	0	2	−	1	4	=
8	=	0	2	2	1	3	2	÷	1	1	=	1	2	4
1	1	÷	1	1	=	1	2	+	9	5	−	=	x	6
6	0	6	÷	3	÷	7	8	0	1	9	7	5	5	2
8	8	÷	1	1	=	8	4	7	+	5	x	+	9	4
4	÷	−	x	5	+	7	7	x	2	3	−	÷	−	3
1	6	4	+	x	5	5	−	5	7	0	8	1	0	+

PAGE 45

4	x	2	4	÷	6	5	2	8	8	÷	0	6	4	0
4	4	0	6	x	4	1	−	1	2	7	8	4	6	÷
÷	x	x	6	9	9	9	2	2	6	5	1	8	2	2
8	4	÷	1	2	=	7	+	1	0	0	9	÷	3	1
7	6	1	7	7	1	3	2	÷	1	2	=	1	1	2
2	0	−	2	+	3	8	7	−	7	+	2	2	x	0
÷	÷	0	3	÷	5	1	3	9	÷	1	4	=	0	÷
1	1	3	0	−	+	7	4	1	=	5	x	4	−	1
2	2	2	5	+	+	8	3	2	4	÷	1	2	=	2
=	=	−	1	9	=	−	1	2	÷	1	2	=	1	=
6	5	+	+	2	5	÷	6	8	−	1	÷	5	8	1
2	5	3	1	0	4	1	0	8	÷	1	2	=	9	0
2	−	÷	6	4	x	−	7	3	6	÷	1	2	=	3
−	6	8	1	0	4	0	8	2	7	6	1	4	÷	4
9	+	2	9	0	4	6	0	0	−	2	1	7	5	6

Solutions

PAGE 46

2	6	1	5	7	+	6	7	8	4	÷	1	2	=	7
x	÷	5	1	9	÷	=	1	÷	+	÷	+	4	4	0
7	÷	8	5	6	1	7	x	2	÷	7	2	+	2	4
4	8	4	1	1	2	2	2	5	÷	÷	1	x	2	8
+	1	4	÷	2	1	+	0	–	1	1	3	=	6	3
3	0	7	7	6	÷	3	3	x	4	3	2	0	4	7
5	7	+	3	÷	1	5	x	–	x	1	÷	=	9	–
4	8	–	4	9	1	÷	4	8	÷	0	1	4	1	5
6	8	4	8	+	=	6	1	4	2	5	2	8	x	1
9	7	÷	+	9	1	=	2	9	3	7	=	÷	7	9
4	3	3	÷	1	1	=	3	6	6	8	1	1	÷	÷
8	8	÷	1	1	=	8	8	2	3	4	1	2	0	–
5	7	÷	÷	6	–	4	6	0	5	7	7	=	8	3
0	8	1	1	4	4	÷	1	2	=	1	2	4	2	0
0	1	1	1	0	÷	1	1	=	1	0	4	9	1	+

PAGE 47

÷	3	0	9	8	7	3	3	1	8	7	5	6	4	+
+	x	0	+	0	0	–	2	2	+	7	2	9	4	x
5	+	9	8	6	7	–	2	2	0	5	+	6	÷	+
0	4	+	9	7	6	3	1	÷	+	1	6	÷	1	–
5	5	8	9	÷	0	4	6	1	5	4	0	1	1	÷
7	5	6	7	2	1	+	5	1	÷	1	÷	2	=	x
2	2	÷	–	0	5	1	5	=	=	3	1	=	4	1
÷	8	7	1	2	3	–	=	2	1	–	2	8	8	3
1	3	0	5	1	x	5	1	9	0	0	=	+	4	2
2	6	6	–	4	=	÷	2	8	8	9	5	x	1	÷
=	3	8	x	2	0	5	3	6	÷	1	2	=	3	1
6	÷	1	9	2	4	+	4	7	1	7	x	1	0	1
6	6	÷	1	1	=	6	3	4	2	4	8	9	5	=
+	8	4	+	–	x	–	2	+	=	4	÷	–	2	1
6	8	9	1	8	–	5	2	6	9	8	7	7	÷	2

PAGE 48

7	3	1	9	4	4	8	3	7	x	3	7	8	1	4
7	9	÷	3	7	7	5	7	–	x	2	3	4	2	–
7	x	7	=	4	9	x	5	3	8	2	–	7	1	2
–	0	2	3	3	÷	5	=	0	4	9	8	9	=	1
0	0	5	÷	–	1	9	7	÷	1	0	3	4	1	3
5	2	=	5	x	5	1	3	–	9	9	4	5	1	8
8	8	3	3	1	3	÷	2	1	4	1	–	1	x	6
8	9	x	3	x	7	7	0	6	=	x	0	1	1	3
x	–	1	x	1	8	7	1	2	4	x	4	9	1	5
–	4	8	0	=	0	=	1	x	1	5	6	1	8	+
8	6	=	2	1	4	x	9	0	1	÷	x	1	3	4
2	=	9	4	x	2	5	=	+	–	2	6	5	2	–
5	8	x	4	1	2	1	1	2	6	2	=	4	÷	4
9	x	9	x	8	0	=	5	7	–	7	3	9	7	0
1	8	3	7	0	–	3	4	4	4	7	6	5	5	9

PAGE 49

x	x	–	9	4	6	7	2	1	–	÷	9	9	x	4
x	1	3	4	4	3	9	2	0	6	9	=	3	x	3
2	1	5	4	0	8	1	6	+	1	5	6	1	2	1
4	÷	3	9	6	=	8	7	4	=	4	÷	7	2	5
2	2	6	2	1	1	5	2	5	4	6	=	8	x	8
5	+	0	1	1	4	÷	5	7	x	3	2	2	–	3
0	–	x	5	4	=	2	x	2	4	=	0	0	8	0
0	1	÷	9	2	÷	1	4	1	x	6	7	3	–	5
1	x	8	x	–	=	9	2	4	0	x	5	9	–	–
=	+	x	9	8	3	5	4	5	÷	6	–	2	6	8
0	÷	2	=	x	x	1	x	9	+	9	5	+	÷	9
1	8	4	8	1	1	8	–	5	9	4	=	7	x	7
x	1	x	1	=	1	x	0	6	7	5	4	8	2	x
0	x	9	6	x	6	6	2	4	8	–	2	1	9	0
1	1	2	x	1	2	=	1	4	4	0	9	2	1	–

PAGE 50

1	–	x	3	x	x	–	3	+	+	4	–	1	+	+
5	9	8	6	1	3	=	4	4	4	4	9	0	1	6
3	9	–	8	÷	2	+	7	÷	1	=	7	2	6	1
÷	x	+	5	÷	6	8	2	1	2	8	0	5	7	x
8	0	5	6	–	7	x	6	4	÷	–	1	÷	x	1
0	9	0	=	1	7	+	6	8	2	2	2	5	5	2
x	8	5	8	1	5	7	4	7	=	+	x	=	=	x
–	0	5	2	4	5	5	7	1	6	–	2	5	3	5
6	–	3	6	5	8	8	÷	÷	0	+	=	9	5	=
3	2	1	1	=	1	7	–	5	1	–	2	3	–	6
0	÷	1	2	=	9	x	–	0	=	4	4	4	3	0
2	8	÷	2	7	÷	0	2	4	4	1	3	0	6	2
2	6	x	1	0	=	6	0	0	9	5	1	÷	1	3
1	9	x	2	2	8	0	x	–	6	1	x	0	9	8
8	3	2	5	8	÷	0	÷	–	x	9	6	3	÷	1

PAGE 51

8	x	–	+	8	2	7	3	5	3	0	÷	5	=	6
7	7	1	3	x	+	9	2	2	1	8	6	7	4	÷
5	1	2	0	8	1	=	2	6	2	7	÷	–	6	1
2	÷	2	=	1	5	8	x	1	0	=	8	0	2	1
–	+	5	x	x	9	1	÷	2	÷	0	7	6	1	x
8	2	0	5	4	1	–	9	9	1	3	1	÷	2	1
2	÷	3	1	0	4	0	÷	1	0	=	4	9	1	0
2	1	8	÷	1	7	÷	9	÷	=	4	9	=	x	=
x	x	+	1	1	÷	÷	0	4	1	8	1	4	2	1
2	1	0	÷	5	=	2	0	6	2	x	2	1	6	1
=	4	4	0	5	7	1	x	8	1	7	3	8	÷	0
4	6	4	x	1	x	7	5	1	5	1	3	÷	8	÷
7	6	8	4	2	2	5	1	3	4	–	0	2	8	+
0	0	4	+	7	=	7	5	–	2	9	–	=	0	5
÷	1	2	1	+	x	8	0	4	+	9	2	9	3	÷

PAGE 52

4	+	8	4	4	÷	+	4	–	9	8	2	4	3	3
0	5	3	0	3	–	+	+	÷	÷	1	9	0	+	–
÷	5	6	2	4	÷	4	=	6	6	5	7	3	0	÷
4	9	1	+	2	4	4	6	2	–	7	0	x	4	9
=	5	2	0	x	5	0	5	6	=	0	1	8	–	8
1	0	x	3	=	3	0	6	4	0	–	7	5	÷	5
0	1	4	4	9	6	÷	÷	–	4	0	9	6	2	6
8	0	=	7	=	0	8	x	5	0	2	9	+	9	4
–	7	4	8	4	2	3	4	8	6	1	x	3	=	3
x	4	8	÷	x	÷	0	7	4	+	1	8	6	7	3
x	6	7	1	÷	5	4	1	4	÷	6	5	÷	x	x
6	+	1	x	1	9	3	+	9	7	4	2	3	9	4
5	3	6	1	8	÷	3	=	6	1	6	=	=	÷	=
2	4	x	4	=	1	6	4	0	2	+	4	1	9	1
÷	0	1	–	x	–	4	–	x	5	4	9	2	1	2

PAGE 53

1	5	÷	3	=	5	1	5	3	+	7	x	2	2	+
0	1	0	8	2	÷	3	3	8	x	3	1	1	6	1
2	0	÷	6	1	4	3	=	6	+	÷	1	–	7	1
2	3	+	0	1	7	4	3	x	9	6	x	–	÷	5
–	4	÷	6	4	÷	x	2	3	2	5	4	+	3	7
2	9	÷	1	2	2	8	6	=	6	–	=	8	6	3
2	÷	2	3	+	+	0	–	1	x	9	4	4	2	6
7	x	8	3	=	0	6	2	8	2	0	4	2	3	9
÷	4	1	1	1	8	÷	x	1	5	÷	3	=	1	0
3	6	÷	0	9	–	3	4	7	÷	=	3	+	2	3
=	8	0	7	÷	3	=	=	3	4	x	+	6	÷	9
9	9	–	x	x	–	2	8	x	2	5	7	7	4	0
+	2	–	3	0	÷	2	8	1	2	4	1	4	=	8
x	2	9	+	x	–	5	–	–	4	9	3	0	3	4
9	7	8	9	x	4	=	3	6	÷	3	4	3	8	8

PAGE 54

9	0	1	7	7	x	÷	3	+	8	3	7	÷	1	1
5	3	0	÷	6	=	5	–	8	÷	x	4	–	5	2
1	7	x	x	x	3	x	5	6	2	6	3	0	5	+
7	0	x	4	3	4	8	9	+	2	=	x	x	7	3
5	7	x	7	8	x	7	=	5	6	1	0	x	2	x
+	÷	9	7	=	6	1	9	7	5	8	8	9	÷	5
+	÷	3	2	=	4	3	–	–	5	=	x	6	6	x
4	1	+	3	6	7	9	3	2	7	6	÷	x	=	1
2	2	÷	0	3	8	0	7	÷	=	6	3	6	1	0
7	x	4	4	÷	8	3	6	7	x	2	x	=	2	7
2	7	9	2	7	8	5	÷	x	+	3	2	3	÷	2
6	=	+	9	=	+	2	9	5	x	x	1	6	5	1
0	8	3	8	9	4	8	–	3	0	8	7	–	5	4
0	4	÷	4	x	3	5	1	4	6	÷	+	3	2	+
2	4	–	3	5	0	6	0	÷	6	=	1	0	0	x

Solutions

PAGE 55

7	x	7	=	4	9	3	÷	9	5	0	3	2	÷	9
7	–	–	x	1	–	5	8	1	+	1	2	5	–	0
8	3	8	x	7	2	2	8	8	2	x	x	x	3	9
6	5	1	÷	7	4	÷	x	0	6	x	0	x	x	0
6	9	0	1	5	5	7	6	5	9	4	6	5	8	÷
÷	7	0	1	3	3	6	5	=	0	x	8	=	8	÷
6	÷	6	1	1	7	+	1	8	2	7	x	3	7	6
=	4	–	2	=	3	8	–	4	+	=	6	–	5	2
1	2	6	6	6	5	+	0	÷	x	2	=	0	5	5
1	+	÷	=	6	4	6	2	7	–	8	4	0	–	9
÷	2	7	4	5	0	5	5	=	2	3	8	7	9	0
4	x	8	=	8	5	4	0	1	–	3	5	+	9	8
9	–	6	6	1	–	9	x	2	2	8	÷	7	=	4
4	x	3	8	1	8	÷	6	=	3	4	+	8	+	0
9	÷	1	9	÷	–	6	1	0	8	1	0	x	9	4

PAGE 56

6	3	÷	9	=	7	0	÷	8	2	2	9	–	7	7
x	1	0	3	5	4	x	+	6	5	4	5	8	4	5
5	–	8	9	5	2	4	0	4	–	x	1	–	0	–
6	–	x	=	8	6	÷	+	2	÷	4	5	1	÷	5
3	0	9	+	5	+	÷	4	x	7	7	=	2	8	9
7	x	=	6	7	x	6	7	–	0	9	–	x	=	6
6	5	5	8	9	5	8	8	÷	÷	0	7	8	5	2
6	+	2	+	8	+	9	=	0	2	÷	6	=	1	4
–	x	–	0	x	9	0	9	4	2	2	x	9	7	0
2	8	0	x	8	2	9	x	÷	0	x	3	6	3	4
9	9	÷	9	=	1	1	4	8	6	7	÷	8	x	5
4	–	+	6	6	÷	x	5	5	5	–	3	8	8	÷
2	8	0	4	4	3	5	+	1	7	2	÷	8	=	9
3	2	2	8	8	5	5	8	9	8	9	4	8	2	=
6	–	5	5	7	x	8	=	5	6	9	5	6	4	5

PAGE 57

4	x	9	=	3	6	6	5	1	0	–	5	4	6	–
8	1	2	4	÷	8	=	3	7	9	x	=	1	+	+
7	1	4	1	3	5	5	9	2	1	8	2	+	0	5
5	x	7	x	1	–	3	2	8	÷	9	7	5	5	÷
9	8	0	8	÷	–	2	–	2	÷	9	3	7	x	7
6	=	x	÷	2	8	0	3	9	x	8	=	7	2	6
÷	8	6	8	5	9	9	1	8	–	9	4	x	+	4
8	8	6	6	=	9	–	9	8	–	3	=	x	9	÷
=	2	2	9	–	x	4	8	÷	8	=	6	1	x	8
1	7	x	+	+	2	8	8	8	9	5	8	4	8	=
2	0	4	1	4	1	6	–	x	4	5	x	1	2	8
1	8	÷	9	=	2	9	+	7	+	+	8	–	x	0
5	8	4	5	5	x	÷	5	6	4	x	=	7	–	0
2	+	+	4	7	x	6	x	+	4	3	6	÷	2	8
5	÷	–	4	4	8	+	8	2	9	–	4	–	7	5

PAGE 58

–	6	1	7	0	8	7	4	6	0	÷	1	2	=	5
1	1	3	7	x	+	0	5	+	+	6	0	3	–	3
5	8	2	5	3	x	x	÷	x	4	1	x	4	8	x
1	x	÷	2	6	2	0	x	6	1	6	1	3	+	2
1	÷	1	+	8	2	6	6	2	0	1	1	9	–	6
x	8	2	4	4	8	÷	7	+	–	1	=	8	9	5
1	+	=	9	7	7	÷	7	3	1	3	1	5	9	6
1	8	1	8	+	3	7	3	1	8	4	1	1	5	6
=	0	1	2	x	=	=	+	9	4	2	0	–	7	2
1	6	8	2	2	1	7	0	8	÷	5	4	5	5	÷
2	2	÷	1	1	=	2	=	4	3	0	9	3	2	4
1	3	÷	x	6	÷	2	=	2	4	÷	1	2	=	2
–	4	3	–	1	1	2	5	9	4	8	8	2	9	÷
8	0	+	6	x	6	3	2	6	6	÷	1	1	=	6
3	+	0	7	3	6	1	9	9	3	0	7	+	6	2

PAGE 59

1	1	÷	÷	+	x	x	1	7	0	6	8	–	÷	–
1	3	9	2	2	2	9	9	4	9	=	6	+	x	6
4	2	0	9	5	+	4	1	3	1	6	0	0	6	–
1	÷	÷	1	x	6	3	7	1	4	1	6	+	0	3
1	1	2	0	1	8	1	÷	1	=	–	7	2	3	1
x	1	9	4	2	5	8	+	1	3	5	7	4	–	0
1	=	5	–	=	8	9	1	4	6	5	9	–	3	8
1	1	÷	+	6	8	÷	9	x	1	1	=	9	9	÷
=	2	6	÷	0	0	0	+	5	4	7	+	–	4	1
1	2	x	3	1	6	2	÷	5	x	3	+	3	4	2
2	0	1	1	9	x	7	x	7	1	9	8	5	÷	=
1	1	x	1	2	=	1	3	2	2	7	8	2	1	9
3	6	÷	1	2	=	3	6	7	=	5	÷	4	1	÷
2	–	x	3	1	+	2	5	5	4	+	6	5	=	7
÷	0	3	4	3	–	3	4	+	8	7	+	2	4	4

PAGE 60

+	1	6	0	7	6	–	2	8	0	0	3	3	4	÷
8	6	+	1	–	5	÷	5	÷	8	+	1	–	4	6
0	6	9	0	6	1	7	1	0	+	0	–	4	2	–
+	7	4	6	1	4	1	7	2	4	x	+	6	1	8
8	1	9	9	=	9	x	1	1	=	5	8	x	2	7
0	÷	8	2	+	9	=	7	8	4	3	–	6	+	1
2	x	+	x	÷	3	9	6	5	4	=	x	8	3	8
5	8	9	8	x	÷	4	0	6	9	=	4	7	–	3
5	5	4	4	3	+	5	2	+	9	4	2	x	–	–
x	–	0	–	x	5	1	5	2	6	5	=	1	1	0
6	÷	0	6	=	7	x	2	x	x	6	2	7	x	9
=	6	5	5	x	8	3	7	0	2	3	=	8	x	4
3	–	x	3	=	9	x	1	0	=	9	0	7	÷	7
0	1	5	4	8	9	+	–	2	1	x	4	5	6	3
1	6	0	8	7	+	÷	+	÷	2	3	9	+	1	1

PAGE 61

7	8	9	6	–	3	6	8	x	6	2	3	3	8	8
6	5	4	3	6	=	7	x	9	4	x	6	x	1	8
–	÷	–	8	1	0	4	2	1	9	2	6	3	1	2
4	5	7	1	0	1	5	2	=	9	0	2	8	2	8
6	3	2	=	x	9	x	2	2	1	=	4	x	3	9
2	5	2	6	8	6	7	+	3	8	9	0	8	3	2
1	7	÷	x	=	9	7	1	6	4	0	1	–	7	+
1	8	5	3	8	0	2	=	5	x	4	6	1	+	+
7	÷	÷	2	0	0	0	1	4	7	6	1	6	1	9
6	2	0	5	3	1	1	+	9	–	–	4	7	x	=
5	6	x	÷	=	6	x	–	1	4	÷	0	2	x	1
0	4	9	0	+	9	1	+	+	1	0	=	5	9	x
x	8	1	4	6	x	6	=	3	6	1	2	+	6	9
2	x	5	=	1	0	3	–	5	8	–	8	2	7	6
1	1	+	6	7	5	4	6	7	4	2	x	3	=	6

PAGE 62

x	5	–	1	x	4	=	4	3	9	0	x	9	÷	–
6	x	1	9	7	÷	6	6	3	4	÷	6	7	÷	9
1	÷	2	9	7	0	=	2	x	9	=	1	8	3	÷
8	6	2	0	–	9	7	2	+	9	1	÷	0	7	x
x	2	+	4	x	4	=	1	6	x	8	2	4	6	7
7	x	2	7	1	÷	4	1	3	9	6	x	5	+	1
=	8	x	9	=	7	2	x	x	7	–	4	x	4	0
5	6	–	3	–	7	8	4	6	x	8	4	7	÷	x
6	6	0	9	9	x	8	=	7	2	1	9	=	÷	4
3	x	4	=	2	4	4	4	=	+	8	4	3	6	=
8	3	1	x	8	÷	÷	4	+	–	4	6	5	6	4
7	x	6	8	6	7	x	1	–	9	3	1	0	+	0
9	2	7	4	1	7	6	÷	4	5	8	9	x	x	x
–	+	x	2	7	5	+	7	+	0	1	+	5	9	6
1	1	x	9	=	9	9	5	3	9	0	1	0	5	1

PAGE 63

8	8	4	x	9	=	3	6	2	7	8	0	9	0	5
7	4	6	÷	x	2	8	x	0	1	8	–	0	7	3
1	1	–	÷	1	÷	+	7	9	+	÷	–	8	1	4
2	0	x	6	1	7	6	=	2	1	7	4	x	6	9
–	x	5	–	=	x	÷	4	0	6	7	2	5	3	0
8	2	5	0	9	3	2	2	2	–	5	–	=	÷	9
4	=	÷	–	9	=	8	0	1	9	6	5	4	8	x
6	2	x	1	=	2	6	7	1	6	6	1	0	÷	1
6	0	1	6	x	1	1	x	1	1	=	1	2	1	1
8	5	0	+	3	8	0	9	6	2	1	6	x	+	=
1	9	7	1	÷	6	=	1	x	7	x	2	6	÷	8
3	9	4	÷	4	–	0	8	8	8	3	3	5	9	9
4	x	7	=	2	8	0	4	x	1	0	=	4	0	1
7	x	2	=	1	4	+	6	8	1	3	–	x	x	x
5	–	5	9	8	4	3	8	8	8	+	9	8	4	7

Solutions

PAGE 64

3	3	−	3	÷	−	−	6	4	4	3	+	2	4	6
5	x	7	2	÷	9	0	1	9	−	÷	4	4	7	0
2	3	7	8	x	9	=	7	2	+	6	9	0	5	0
2	4	1	=	2	7	x	5	=	3	5	8	1	x	5
8	+	8	0	2	9	8	x	1	1	2	1	3	6	x
5	9	6	3	1	1	÷	4	4	=	2	0	6	=	1
2	5	3	5	2	1	3	2	7	3	5	x	7	3	1
9	8	5	8	0	3	4	x	8	6	8	5	6	0	=
9	5	4	1	=	1	4	0	3	6	÷	=	x	5	5
0	2	−	1	4	3	3	7	2	−	7	5	9	3	5
2	4	1	x	3	x	÷	x	9	x	1	0	4	÷	6
1	x	+	4	3	1	5	8	9	÷	−	−	7	+	7
3	x	3	5	4	4	2	=	7	9	7	1	9	−	4
4	2	1	=	÷	x	+	5	2	2	0	4	5	0	3
6	÷	−	5	6	3	6	6	=	0	7	8	0	5	4

PAGE 65

0	÷	+	4	7	2	÷	6	x	0	5	2	4	0	+
9	8	2	÷	1	4	7	−	8	1	5	9	7	6	0
0	6	0	x	−	6	8	5	8	9	x	+	7	6	9
0	4	+	−	0	3	÷	2	5	3	1	8	x	9	−
−	0	3	8	÷	x	9	1	2	7	9	0	6	5	8
0	x	+	x	6	6	6	2	1	−	5	0	=	0	+
0	5	7	+	1	=	7	9	3	4	x	9	4	x	8
9	3	8	2	x	1	+	÷	8	6	3	x	2	9	x
x	0	4	−	4	8	=	2	÷	9	=	3	8	x	6
6	3	1	6	2	x	4	3	6	x	1	=	6	8	÷
=	6	0	7	3	x	1	=	3	÷	5	2	1	=	3
5	+	3	2	9	8	÷	−	x	4	x	7	5	7	0
4	8	x	+	+	−	8	7	x	4	=	2	8	2	1
−	9	−	3	+	0	−	3	8	1	4	x	2	=	8
1	0	x	2	=	2	0	2	x	5	÷	9	4	0	1

PAGE 66

9	0	7	9	4	3	3	+	+	÷	3	2	0	5	2
+	÷	9	=	1	+	−	6	9	3	4	5	0	9	6
4	2	x	1	2	4	x	x	−	8	x	6	0	3	=
+	−	x	÷	9	7	2	3	0	1	=	4	÷	0	4
2	1	5	9	4	2	6	8	÷	3	+	−	4	3	÷
8	x	0	8	5	÷	5	5	0	5	6	+	x	x	4
9	8	7	÷	6	8	−	−	7	2	x	+	+	0	2
5	−	5	=	1	5	8	6	8	+	6	9	2	9	8
7	=	6	0	4	=	6	9	8	7	3	1	0	0	7
5	2	9	9	8	÷	1	3	÷	3	÷	7	÷	7	x
0	=	3	9	6	−	8	0	8	+	x	÷	5	1	9
5	5	1	÷	8	−	−	2	=	2	+	0	=	5	x
5	÷	3	7	9	7	x	−	1	5	4	9	4	+	4
4	0	x	5	8	x	0	÷	1	=	1	÷	1	1	5
9	1	x	x	1	0	0	÷	1	0	=	1	0	+	5

PAGE 67

9	8	−	÷	0	1	9	1	0	4	8	÷	6	=	8
7	3	6	3	÷	7	=	9	5	5	÷	5	−	÷	0
8	3	6	÷	6	=	6	÷	6	2	5	3	+	1	3
4	1	4	9	9	8	5	3	6	6	1	4	0	5	−
9	=	1	÷	9	=	4	2	÷	1	=	−	4	5	−
8	2	1	÷	9	6	6	8	9	=	1	+	x	÷	=
÷	8	+	3	x	4	=	3	7	6	1	9	2	9	x
÷	8	8	3	6	7	5	x	5	3	÷	7	=	8	1
÷	5	1	÷	0	3	÷	6	4	4	1	0	2	=	6
9	4	4	3	1	2	÷	3	=	4	1	x	4	9	+
4	+	−	=	+	6	5	+	1	÷	8	1	8	÷	+
x	3	=	1	1	÷	=	3	0	3	2	1	9	2	7
0	7	8	1	+	2	0	9	+	+	8	+	4	7	x
÷	0	0	5	2	0	7	4	÷	6	5	x	6	9	4
8	−	0	1	=	7	÷	0	7	x	8	3	÷	7	4

PAGE 68

9	3	4	÷	7	5	+	9	9	4	7	6	2	1	8
5	3	x	6	2	=	4	2	5	+	=	8	6	7	−
4	3	9	6	÷	5	0	9	+	6	9	1	0	7	÷
5	÷	9	9	8	÷	7	1	4	3	5	0	÷	4	x
0	3	+	−	=	5	7	0	=	6	÷	3	2	4	0
9	=	3	÷	9	2	−	7	7	0	1	7	+	0	7
2	1	4	8	÷	x	+	−	4	1	1	3	9	=	2
9	1	+	÷	2	5	5	7	=	7	4	÷	5	4	x
6	7	−	+	7	5	8	1	0	7	7	÷	0	7	1
2	1	÷	7	=	3	1	+	3	5	5	+	0	0	9
÷	0	÷	9	8	÷	÷	0	2	3	=	1	8	0	1
8	7	−	9	1	7	4	÷	÷	8	4	9	6	4	3
0	x	1	2	7	4	−	−	4	2	÷	÷	÷	−	3
8	+	1	2	0	+	4	9	=	5	0	3	2	5	÷
4	2	0	2	9	1	0	÷	8	8	2	÷	2	9	4

PAGE 69

1	+	÷	1	6	x	7	5	0	x	4	9	−	x	2
8	4	1	1	6	3	3	1	+	6	9	4	9	6	−
9	+	1	+	6	÷	+	6	0	−	9	8	2	7	8
2	+	=	÷	7	8	9	÷	3	÷	3	3	4	+	6
1	+	3	1	−	9	9	÷	1	7	1	+	÷	7	+
÷	3	÷	3	x	÷	2	6	1	7	9	0	3	÷	2
7	÷	3	6	÷	2	=	3	=	9	4	4	=	1	5
=	x	3	4	9	2	8	9	−	2	=	6	8	1	4
3	x	2	8	=	5	÷	9	0	1	÷	2	1	3	=
−	7	9	9	9	3	6	0	1	4	2	7	x	÷	8
5	2	÷	7	6	−	1	÷	5	2	8	4	+	9	÷
0	8	5	9	+	−	4	4	6	0	9	÷	3	+	2
1	8	7	5	0	4	6	4	÷	8	=	8	3	0	3
÷	0	9	0	÷	x	5	9	7	6	8	5	6	+	÷
÷	1	+	7	1	3	−	3	5	=	7	÷	5	3	+

PAGE 70

1	+	3	8	x	3	5	2	9	2	3	1	0	÷	3
5	3	=	2	÷	6	x	1	0	1	=	6	÷	0	6
2	−	4	6	6	9	9	1	7	0	x	6	6	+	1
7	1	2	4	x	+	+	=	4	1	8	1	4	4	8
9	8	2	7	1	÷	8	8	1	2	=	−	4	3	6
2	3	9	÷	+	4	1	÷	=	7	2	4	2	−	2
x	6	+	6	2	2	÷	8	7	x	1	4	0	9	8
2	x	8	+	7	=	÷	8	4	÷	÷	2	5	8	1
6	4	x	2	+	6	6	1	9	5	6	−	2	−	6
6	0	9	1	1	=	4	÷	4	4	9	7	8	4	2
x	=	2	÷	2	1	−	x	0	8	6	1	5	0	5
−	5	6	+	3	3	7	−	0	3	6	÷	÷	4	2
6	4	0	÷	4	=	1	0	2	3	9	5	9	6	÷
8	0	÷	9	6	3	7	1	+	=	=	−	÷	2	6
7	=	5	÷	5	3	6	7	5	4	x	+	7	3	+

PAGE 71

4	2	÷	6	=	7	2	−	7	÷	7	5	7	2	4
2	−	+	1	0	8	1	0	7	5	+	−	8	6	3
0	÷	0	−	8	7	8	6	7	2	−	+	6	9	1
1	1	=	2	÷	2	2	5	4	7	÷	+	=	4	x
4	−	7	1	7	6	6	2	0	x	÷	9	1	7	4
3	÷	4	6	2	÷	÷	+	2	1	÷	7	=	3	4
x	1	9	1	5	0	5	0	5	1	=	6	÷	8	÷
−	6	−	7	1	5	2	=	8	4	x	5	8	+	+
÷	7	5	x	=	2	=	=	1	7	1	9	÷	+	7
2	−	÷	5	0	0	÷	8	2	1	0	5	7	0	9
8	÷	x	1	1	5	1	3	÷	÷	÷	7	2	÷	5
7	1	0	6	7	6	4	÷	=	0	4	5	0	9	9
9	6	7	x	7	2	−	3	0	4	4	7	5	5	3
−	8	=	4	÷	2	3	÷	2	7	÷	7	2	9	6
8	+	6	6	2	3	+	1	2	÷	6	=	2	9	9

PAGE 72

3	3	3	÷	8	−	4	4	0	=	6	8	0	0	2
x	=	6	3	÷	4	=	0	7	x	9	6	7	5	5
8	÷	4	2	4	0	2	0	6	2	2	3	1	2	1
9	4	4	÷	3	8	÷	2	6	=	+	+	1	5	1
+	5	3	=	2	7	8	5	0	3	+	=	8	0	1
3	6	5	−	=	1	1	8	0	9	6	1	3	4	2
÷	x	1	1	x	5	=	5	5	÷	7	5	−	÷	=
6	7	0	0	8	8	3	−	2	8	9	4	÷	÷	7
0	8	x	x	4	÷	7	7	=	5	6	0	x	8	x
9	6	4	3	−	4	6	9	3	x	9	5	6	3	3
5	1	2	=	x	x	÷	=	9	2	0	3	5	1	3
7	9	3	3	0	2	0	=	3	÷	9	7	4	7	5
+	8	4	0	7	x	5	+	÷	1	6	9	4	÷	0
5	5	3	x	4	4	x	6	7	4	4	x	1	=	4
2	0	8	−	2	6	x	0	9	9	1	0	1	4	0

Solutions

PAGE 73

7	÷	6	1	8	1	+	1	1	1	x	6	=	6	4
8	=	3	9	1	2	1	7	÷	6	7	x	9	4	9
0	9	7	+	7	7	−	1	1	÷	÷	+	x	9	÷
÷	6	8	=	1	÷	x	8	0	x	0	4	4	1	7
÷	−	9	8	1	7	÷	8	÷	÷	−	0	=	+	=
9	x	6	5	−	6	1	7	=	7	1	÷	3	4	7
8	=	3	−	=	−	x	5	÷	5	+	=	7	6	2
1	8	÷	3	7	5	5	−	6	0	6	4	1	3	3
1	7	1	1	x	5	=	5	5	7	+	2	3	0	=
=	0	=	−	4	8	4	2	÷	9	7	5	+	9	÷
3	÷	2	4	=	9	1	3	8	5	8	x	÷	−	1
÷	5	x	7	÷	2	3	=	4	x	8	3	3	x	+
3	7	÷	+	÷	8	7	2	4	−	−	7	1	0	0
3	6	5	7	÷	7	2	7	4	2	=	4	x	6	0
5	8	8	1	4	4	0	0	6	6	6	÷	0	3	0

PAGE 74

4	1	4	4	÷	1	2	=	1	2	4	x	6	6	−
8	1	3	7	4	4	9	−	3	7	4	3	0	8	2
x	1	+	3	4	2	6	=	0	1	÷	0	6	=	3
5	÷	4	5	−	3	=	5	÷	5	1	8	4	2	−
+	8	7	2	8	÷	7	4	3	9	4	0	0	÷	1
2	1	7	4	8	4	6	−	=	5	4	+	1	6	x
−	1	5	3	2	9	x	x	1	6	x	5	=	1	+
7	9	=	=	=	8	7	÷	0	−	8	1	7	5	=
÷	0	6	2	+	7	−	−	4	x	3	=	÷	4	4
7	x	+	2	x	+	÷	0	1	−	x	3	0	+	−
4	5	=	9	x	6	8	1	−	7	1	x	7	1	1
+	+	+	6	2	9	=	8	2	6	1	=	÷	+	−
4	9	5	7	8	8	2	9	1	3	=	x	1	−	÷
8	2	2	÷	8	5	8	1	7	1	3	3	3	6	2
9	−	0	1	=	x	3	0	7	+	3	÷	+	+	2

PAGE 75

8	2	x	9	4	4	2	7	1	8	÷	8	=	1	1
0	4	3	9	4	4	4	4	8	5	−	4	2	9	−
÷	x	x	1	6	=	1	÷	0	7	9	3	7	4	2
1	−	9	÷	1	÷	7	4	6	−	6	4	x	4	0
0	1	=	2	9	0	+	x	3	x	6	1	5	6	5
=	2	2	8	9	=	x	x	7	4	÷	=	3	3	7
8	1	7	4	1	÷	4	1	+	4	6	7	6	+	0
5	=	−	3	5	4	4	÷	1	0	=	x	8	2	4
x	4	7	0	3	5	6	−	6	=	1	2	+	7	6
7	x	6	3	+	÷	2	2	8	3	1	+	2	x	6
÷	3	8	÷	3	9	−	7	0	−	6	1	2	1	2
÷	0	8	÷	÷	=	4	5	÷	1	8	5	0	1	5
7	x	x	4	4	5	4	3	7	+	1	2	9	=	5
5	1	2	x	5	=	+	3	x	8	9	0	x	7	8
÷	1	8	5	+	÷	2	÷	÷	4	0	8	6	7	5

PAGE 76

−	1	6	9	7	3	7	3	x	7	1	÷	9	2	3
8	=	1	x	8	0	1	5	1	7	8	1	+	8	9
5	4	7	8	−	1	9	x	5	4	1	0	1	9	8
5	4	2	2	x	9	=	1	8	2	÷	÷	2	+	x
+	+	3	=	=	x	1	=	−	8	9	2	8	0	5
6	5	1	−	4	4	4	5	÷	3	=	2	=	5	4
5	3	2	3	3	x	÷	2	x	1	9	÷	1	7	÷
8	2	3	÷	0	2	6	7	x	3	3	8	x	4	6
8	1	6	÷	8	=	2	2	=	x	0	2	5	5	=
5	5	÷	1	1	=	5	x	+	2	÷	5	0	2	9
+	÷	÷	2	5	÷	x	3	3	0	8	7	7	=	2
−	8	5	x	÷	7	5	−	+	7	9	5	6	5	0
2	7	x	7	4	1	1	6	0	0	2	1	2	x	=
4	7	5	7	8	4	x	1	1	=	4	4	2	5	5
9	3	6	=	3	÷	8	1	=	5	÷	5	=	1	1

PAGE 77

−	9	9	8	5	9	x	1	2	=	1	0	8	6	4
8	5	1	9	÷	7	3	=	7	÷	−	3	5	=	6
0	5	6	7	7	7	3	x	x	6	2	2	−	5	1
1	1	x	1	=	1	1	3	1	3	7	8	5	=	1
4	9	8	+	1	0	+	=	2	9	6	÷	3	3	x
7	2	8	1	−	3	x	2	÷	÷	÷	+	8	0	1
9	5	7	x	6	4	3	7	2	3	1	−	0	2	1
6	5	+	−	2	7	÷	9	=	3	5	2	7	1	=
1	+	÷	−	7	=	8	+	6	−	+	=	=	4	1
x	5	8	3	0	5	1	6	÷	1	5	2	÷	x	2
7	2	3	2	0	÷	4	6	x	÷	÷	6	÷	1	1
=	9	7	9	4	÷	8	2	5	2	6	2	4	0	x
7	7	2	4	5	2	5	3	2	3	5	7	−	2	+
0	x	2	3	8	2	−	=	2	4	2	4	5	8	÷
5	4	÷	6	=	9	+	+	6	3	x	4	=	1	2

PAGE 78

2	2	1	3	2	÷	1	1	=	1	2	=	9	x	9
8	1	=	8	5	6	−	6	3	−	3	3	7	4	1
0	7	8	8	2	3	6	0	1	6	5	1	1	+	x
2	+	÷	3	0	−	4	−	1	1	7	2	2	x	6
8	7	8	x	÷	7	7	1	7	8	3	1	1	6	÷
=	5	8	4	8	6	=	6	6	5	x	−	0	8	0
7	3	1	8	9	2	5	7	2	9	2	5	9	x	2
÷	=	+	6	÷	6	3	6	÷	1	=	÷	=	0	=
7	7	+	2	7	÷	x	6	÷	9	6	3	0	9	2
=	x	2	−	=	1	5	x	9	=	4	5	1	0	x
1	5	2	6	2	+	2	7	÷	6	3	5	x	7	0
1	5	x	÷	÷	8	4	÷	÷	1	1	6	9	0	1
=	÷	1	5	4	7	7	÷	1	1	=	7	4	3	÷
8	3	x	1	1	=	3	3	x	÷	x	0	8	0	8
+	÷	1	1	9	0	3	−	6	3	0	6	6	+	−

PAGE 79

0	2	1	9	3	2	x	5	1	6	−	4	÷	7	−
5	0	−	4	+	6	3	5	÷	6	+	4	÷	+	4
3	÷	÷	5	−	9	1	−	7	9	x	÷	9	7	4
=	2	8	4	x	1	9	6	÷	4	0	1	7	6	÷
5	=	x	=	x	4	3	÷	9	1	0	1	3	÷	1
x	1	6	5	+	2	4	=	=	8	8	=	2	0	1
7	0	=	x	1	4	5	0	1	1	5	4	−	−	5
÷	5	4	9	0	8	1	8	x	1	+	x	x	1	−
5	6	8	=	8	÷	4	6	−	9	÷	7	2	1	÷
1	−	7	3	0	8	=	2	−	=	5	3	8	7	0
5	−	2	0	1	÷	÷	5	x	9	x	+	3	4	−
3	9	1	7	7	−	9	5	8	x	0	0	=	9	3
4	1	9	+	4	x	=	6	+	1	6	5	5	3	÷
−	7	−	x	x	÷	5	5	6	+	x	2	7	6	1
7	2	÷	9	=	8	=	1	8	8	5	1	4	1	3

PAGE 80

÷	3	1	6	9	÷	÷	7	9	+	7	4	4	2	5
8	7	2	7	x	6	7	x	2	=	1	4	+	5	−
=	÷	0	9	8	4	8	9	0	8	x	+	7	x	2
1	9	+	+	3	9	=	1	4	0	6	−	0	7	1
3	−	7	−	8	9	0	2	+	2	8	5	÷	=	9
2	9	3	x	9	5	3	3	4	3	4	0	7	3	2
÷	1	x	9	÷	3	x	7	2	9	2	9	=	5	9
1	6	4	6	=	7	1	3	2	2	÷	3	1	9	−
2	÷	3	6	3	+	=	8	4	3	6	x	0	+	x
=	+	÷	7	0	4	3	+	÷	6	=	8	5	x	5
1	8	÷	5	x	6	8	5	8	2	7	+	0	6	÷
1	2	x	8	7	8	−	7	=	4	=	x	2	7	7
1	+	0	8	3	8	=	4	3	x	−	9	3	÷	÷
÷	7	0	5	0	x	÷	5	7	6	2	2	3	7	÷
1	1	x	2	=	2	2	6	6	÷	0	+	+	0	8

PAGE 81

1	5	5	5	0	x	−	+	4	9	9	7	7	9	6
1	9	4	2	6	4	3	0	5	2	9	2	2	5	6
7	÷	1	4	2	÷	8	6	6	x	x	5	−	4	−
1	8	5	9	9	=	8	÷	2	8	8	6	=	4	x
1	2	x	4	8	5	3	=	8	÷	+	5	=	1	÷
x	2	x	x	9	5	0	7	7	=	÷	0	0	1	7
1	3	0	0	6	x	÷	3	8	0	6	9	8	8	2
1	1	1	+	+	7	3	2	2	3	x	+	−	7	6
=	7	7	9	x	9	=	8	1	6	4	8	x	÷	9
1	4	2	0	1	5	1	6	+	÷	=	2	÷	9	0
2	4	6	8	4	−	0	3	5	÷	2	3	7	8	2
1	1	1	−	3	3	9	9	−	6	4	6	5	x	x
8	1	÷	0	0	3	3	8	x	7	1	5	3	6	1
4	4	÷	4	=	1	1	4	2	÷	6	=	7	4	=
1	0	2	2	x	1	9	8	2	9	7	9	8	1	2

Solutions

PAGE 82

2	–	0	2	2	÷	2	=	1	1	0	÷	x	1	5
x	8	4	3	5	6	6	6	5	x	7	=	3	5	9
5	9	4	÷	x	÷	=	x	5	1	–	+	+	6	+
=	1	5	2	4	9	3	8	0	3	7	3	6	1	1
1	8	–	4	÷	÷	–	4	÷	x	5	2	4	5	5
0	9	1	4	2	7	7	–	5	1	6	x	5	2	÷
3	–	5	2	÷	8	=	÷	=	1	÷	9	1	4	÷
x	+	x	x	5	1	5	6	1	=	8	=	4	4	8
4	3	6	7	9	x	–	8	0	3	=	1	x	=	9
3	+	2	=	7	÷	3	6	1	3	7	8	4	2	4
7	3	5	1	4	6	=	0	7	2	x	x	÷	–	8
x	÷	8	4	7	5	3	8	8	4	2	7	2	9	x
1	8	3	8	÷	6	–	x	6	0	3	x	6	÷	3
–	5	0	0	9	1	x	6	x	÷	4	÷	2	4	4
6	–	3	7	3	2	9	÷	÷	7	5	3	0	3	3

PAGE 83

3	6	0	3	6	+	3	5	5	+	5	5	x	7	0
7	2	4	8	7	0	4	=	4	1	0	0	8	0	4
9	÷	0	7	÷	8	1	3	7	x	5	4	–	4	+
8	4	8	3	÷	x	4	x	x	+	3	÷	=	+	0
7	2	9	9	5	0	–	4	3	÷	+	4	2	5	4
0	2	9	÷	÷	–	0	=	=	0	x	–	1	x	9
1	5	÷	0	7	0	8	1	2	1	x	÷	8	3	8
1	+	x	9	3	=	+	2	1	5	2	x	÷	=	9
0	9	1	+	=	1	7	9	9	4	8	2	3	1	–
÷	÷	6	8	9	8	÷	5	5	9	8	8	=	5	3
1	1	8	0	2	5	÷	5	=	5	9	÷	6	0	0
0	+	3	2	x	1	0	=	2	0	7	2	6	3	÷
=	+	4	x	÷	5	1	5	0	–	÷	0	9	–	5
1	1	0	8	5	1	4	7	8	–	7	0	x	0	=
1	6	2	4	2	6	0	1	7	5	8	0	8	2	6

PAGE 84

9	2	+	2	9	7	4	4	4	8	7	=	7	2	0
÷	4	5	+	x	2	8	7	x	7	3	+	x	2	2
1	÷	7	÷	+	x	x	7	x	÷	0	1	7	5	3
–	3	5	4	+	3	3	x	2	1	3	0	=	1	=
5	=	8	9	1	3	x	4	1	–	1	2	4	÷	7
x	8	5	=	4	9	5	1	2	6	9	=	9	6	÷
+	x	5	1	÷	4	=	3	3	=	9	÷	7	2	1
6	5	3	1	7	9	1	8	0	x	–	÷	2	7	2
7	x	1	÷	=	1	5	3	1	6	0	5	÷	x	9
8	x	3	9	2	2	+	3	2	8	–	0	5	0	4
6	7	4	9	–	9	9	4	9	5	=	–	÷	x	2
–	+	–	8	3	x	+	+	8	5	÷	9	7	4	4
8	4	2	1	8	÷	÷	–	7	7	=	=	x	5	4
9	1	7	4	4	6	+	3	3	1	2	+	+	9	5
8	5	1	0	x	3	=	3	0	8	3	7	–	6	2

PAGE 85

x	5	1	+	5	9	7	1	6	6	0	9	0	8	+
0	1	8	0	9	x	9	x	1	3	–	x	2	x	5
7	2	÷	5	8	5	5	9	–	x	4	x	6	9	8
x	7	3	5	1	3	6	2	÷	2	4	2	5	=	0
5	÷	=	÷	1	6	7	4	0	x	0	=	9	7	÷
6	9	6	5	+	6	6	3	÷	4	1	2	4	2	2
+	=	+	=	–	0	2	÷	7	8	–	6	9	4	–
4	3	3	1	1	x	x	+	1	7	=	9	÷	3	–
8	5	2	1	2	5	8	1	5	6	–	8	7	8	4
7	7	1	3	3	1	8	7	5	6	4	4	=	÷	3
7	4	0	=	÷	0	8	÷	÷	5	÷	6	7	6	8
2	5	7	1	5	4	5	6	=	3	8	7	3	7	8
6	x	9	=	5	4	6	6	–	–	8	8	=	7	5
5	6	5	0	÷	–	x	3	3	÷	+	÷	+	8	–
7	x	=	=	4	9	=	4	x	4	=	1	6	0	3

PAGE 86

–	=	8	+	3	3	4	2	8	6	2	x	7	7	4
x	9	8	x	0	2	6	2	3	5	÷	5	=	7	2
2	8	5	1	3	–	0	4	8	7	5	0	x	x	2
2	4	7	0	=	2	7	0	4	6	9	6	8	6	9
÷	3	8	3	8	3	÷	x	1	3	7	=	÷	9	4
7	0	÷	=	2	÷	x	4	x	=	1	6	1	5	9
1	–	9	6	=	x	2	6	=	6	0	2	8	=	9
1	1	9	x	6	4	9	÷	9	8	5	1	1	0	–
6	4	0	5	÷	+	6	=	7	–	=	÷	x	+	+
4	9	7	6	2	3	5	3	1	2	9	2	6	0	x
0	÷	4	7	1	0	0	5	7	8	=	–	÷	6	1
x	7	0	–	6	÷	0	3	3	3	0	9	3	x	÷
9	=	0	+	6	2	9	1	5	–	0	÷	x	1	–
8	7	7	=	0	7	÷	6	9	6	+	3	+	3	1
1	7	5	4	8	0	4	5	+	2	0	5	–	7	÷